DEAD ON HALLOWEEN

VICTORIA MATTSEN CRIME SERIES
BOOK 7

IFEANYI ESIMAI

eISBN: 978-1-63589-805-7
Print ISBN: 978-1-63589-806-4
Audio ISBN: 978-1-63589-807-1

Cover design by coveredbymelinda.com

Get a FREE copy of The Rookie!

Join my Newsletter for updates, giveaways, teasers, and a FREE copy of the
prequel - The Rookie. Click here or scan the QR code.

For Chinwe...Always.
The wind beneath my wings.

ACKNOWLEDGMENTS

My heartfelt gratitude goes out to my family and friends, whose unwavering faith in me fueled this project from the very start.

I also want to extend a special thanks to a group of incredible individuals whose generous spirit has made an indelible impact on this project, and for that, I am forever grateful.

Erik S
Nneka Anaebonam
Craig Martelle
Jenn Davidson
Chinwe Anyamele
Obioha Emezie
Renee
Okechukwu Obua
Romeo Richards
Ikenna Emeghara
Charles Onunkwo
Adaeze

Every one of you has helped shape this journey in your own unique way, and I couldn't be more thankful. Your support has not only made these books a reality but has also inspired me as I continue to tell Detective Vikki Mattsen's story.

To all the readers, thank you for inviting Detective Vikki

Mattsen into your lives. It's been a joy to share this adventure with you.

Here's to the stories yet to be told.

PROLOGUE

Cindy Kent took long, purposeful strides on the pavement, oblivious to her mortality. The bus stop was ten minutes away, and she was running late.

Cars drove past her on the road, their headlights splicing the darkness. Two women approached from the opposite direction. The streetlamp's yellow glow cast eerie shadows on the pavement.

Cindy bared her teeth as she passed them.

The women froze. Their eyes widened.

"Mother of God," said one of them. She made a sign of the cross and pulled the other closer.

Cindy smiled. Her looks were convincing. She checked the time on her phone. Darn. She would have to take a shortcut if she wanted to catch the seven p.m. bus. There was no avoiding it. She took a deep breath and turned into the cemetery.

Cindy walked briskly along the footpath and tried to forget her fears. She thought of why she loved this time of the year. Leaves were turning from green to a golden hue. The crunch of dried leaves underneath her feet was music to her ears. The air was crisp and clean. The faint smell of woodsmoke in the air reminded her that after Halloween came Thanksgiving, then Christmas, her favorite holiday.

She was about to smile when a dark object zigzagged across the air before her. Cindy jumped back. She placed a hand on her chest to calm her pounding heart. "It's only a bat."

She continued along the path.

"Hoot, hoot, hoot." The sound got louder, then stopped.

Cindy gritted her teeth, pulse racing. "You don't scare me, Mr. Owl."

The deeper she went into the cemetery, the fainter the sound of car engines, tooting horns, and car radios got. Eventually, they disappeared, and she was alone in the middle of the cemetery. Her only companions were the whooshing wind, rustling leaves, and scurrying in the dark.

Cindy was isolated from the rest of the world, but was she alone? Rows of tombstones lined both sides of the walkway.

Here she was, surrounded by hundreds of people. But all were as silent as the graves they slept in. Nervous laughter escaped her lips. She'd seen people with picnic baskets on the grass in the past, and they seemed to enjoy themselves. She was so terrified right now that she couldn't imagine how they found it fun.

Cindy walked faster, hypersensitive to every sound. Despite her wearing thermal underwear, a chill traveled down her spine. She pulled her black cloak tighter and cast furtive glances behind her.

She was surrounded by all types of graves, headstones, mausoleums, and statues of angels. The moonlight cast irregular shadows like bodies rising from the ground—grotesque and foreboding.

There seemed to be more mausoleums in this section of the cemetery than others. The biggest one had the word

Crawford embossed on it. Cindy could barely pay her rent. Why someone would build a house to keep a dead body when people were teetering on homelessness was beyond her.

Well, it wasn't a new thing. People had gone to great lengths in the past and spent untold riches to house the dead. The pyramids in Egypt, The Taj Mahal in India, the—

She jerked to her left. What was that? Then to her right. Was that a scraping sound?

Cindy believed that once someone died, that was it. She didn't believe in that afterlife nonsense. But tonight was not the best time to test that theory. Her muscles tightened, ready for her to run if need be.

The sound of traffic got louder. She was getting closer to the other end of the cemetery. Cindy heaved a sigh of relief, rechecked her phone screen, and smiled. Taking the shortcut across the graveyard was worth it. She'd be at the bus stop on time and planned never to walk across the cemetery again, even if she was offered money.

She whirled to the sound of running footsteps behind her. "What the—?"

Something dark lunged at her, knocking the breath out of her.

Cindy screamed and fell to the ground. She struggled to get up, but whatever it was struck her in the head. Pain enveloped her. The sky lit up with a stunning display of glistening stars, similar to a shower of fireworks at night. She was hit again on the head, and everything went dark.

CHAPTER ONE

Vikki was in Ted's apartment, nursing a cup of coffee. Her mind was devoid of any thoughts.

She and Ted were more or less an item now, but Vikki still believed there shouldn't be any public display of affection, especially at the office. When alone, like now, it was okay to show love.

A pumpkin sat on a layer of newspapers on Ted's dining table. Beside it was a carving kit he'd purchased from the grocery store. His cell phone was mounted on a stand. A YouTube video on the screen showed white rice served with pumpkin sauce.

Ted scratched his head. "I don't want to eat pumpkin sauce or learn recipes."

Vikki laughed. "You typed in the wrong keyword. You have to type in how to carve a pumpkin."

Ted followed her recommendation and got the right video. He watched a little, paused it, and picked up the carving knife.

"Why do you want to carve a pumpkin anyway?" Vikki said. "You should have bought one from the store and placed it by your door. It doesn't have to be cut. People will still know you are open for Halloween and knock on your door."

Ted held the handle of the carver and made a circular cut around the pumpkin stem. "Are you anti-Halloween?"

"No, it's overrated. An excuse for adults to misbehave."

"I celebrated when I was younger, but this is the first time I'm participating fully," Ted said. He removed the pumpkin top. "It looks like a cap." He placed it on the newspapers, then proceeded to the next step.

Ted slipped on a pair of latex gloves, stuck his hand into the hole in the pumpkin, and scooped out the seeds and everything inside.

Vikki shook her head. "What about costumes?"

"What about them?"

"Aren't you supposed to dress up as something?"

"I'm thinking of going as a vampire," Ted said. "Maybe we can get a couple's vampire costume."

"You must be joking. Whenever I see a couple in matching outfits on Halloween, I want to arrest them, put them behind bars, and throw away the keys. It's so corny."

Ted laughed. He took a step back and looked at the pumpkin. With a black marker, he drew the jack-o'-lantern's eyes, nose, mouth, and teeth. Next step, he cut out the shapes he'd marked. Vikki watched in fascination as the pumpkin transformed into a jack-o'-lantern.

"You know, whenever you're tired of being a medical examiner, you have another career you can fall back on."

Ted nodded. "Yes, it reminds me of my day job.

A phone rang.

"I think it's you," Ted said.

Vikki walked over to the coffee table where she'd left her phone. She picked it up and looked at the screen. "It's Gomez. He's going to ask me if I'm coming to his party." Vikki tapped the screen. "Mattsen."

Another phone started to ring.

Ted dropped his carving knife, peeled off one glove, and reached for his phone in his jean's back pocket. "Dr. Brandon."

They both hung up at the same time.

Vikki shook her head. "Halloween-related death—this is not right." She scrutinized her turtle-neck gray sweater and blue jeans. It was after hours. No one would care. She sat on the couch and pulled on her suede boots.

"I got the same message," Ted said. He wrapped the pumpkin seeds and innards in newspaper and tossed them into the garbage. He set the carved pumpkin on another newspaper. He washed his hand in the sink. "I'll have to pick up my gear from the office." He shook his head.

Vikki was shrugging on her jacket. "Crime never sleeps, even on Halloween week. I'll see you at the cemetery."

CHAPTER TWO

Vikki parked her white Ford Explorer behind a police cruiser with flashing lights. She got out, felt the chill, and zipped up her jacket. She was glad she had on a sweater, too.

She fished her phone out of her jeans pocket and glanced up and down the street, ready to snap a picture or take a video. Sometimes the doer hung around to admire their handiwork or to confirm they'd done the job satisfactorily.

There was nobody.

The faint smell of coffee and fried food reached her. Maybe a restaurant was close by. That meant people. Someone might have seen something. She scanned the area, searching for a person or a restaurant. Unfortunately, there was nobody or anywhere to eat as far as her eyes could see.

A few lookie-loos driving by slowed down but moved on when there was nothing to see. Police activity was concentrated inside the cemetery, away from prying eyes. Satisfied with the parameter, Vikki approached the entrance. *St. Ives Cemetery* was written on an intricate metalwork archway.

Yellow tape attached to the pillars supporting the arch barred anyone from entering. Officer Vinny Russo was there to ensure that members of the public didn't break the rule. He rubbed his hands together.

"Hello, Russo," Vikki said.

"Victoria, how are you?"

"I'm good. A bit chilly?"

Russo smiled. "Nothing I can't handle."

Officer Vinny Russo was older—one of the few people who called her Victoria. He'd said it was his late mother's name, too. Vikki was about to walk away when she stopped. Russo was one of the officers in the marine unit. They'd worked on a case not too long ago.

Vikki raised an eyebrow. She'd heard that sometimes freshly dug graves filled with water after it rained, or it could seep in from an underwater spring. "Did drowning play a part here too?"

Russo chuckled. "No, but it is a bizarre case. You have to see for yourself."

Vikki glanced ahead at the scene, suddenly eager to get there. "Really? I'll check it out. Why don't you grab your coat from your cruiser before you catch a cold? No civilian in their right mind would think of crossing that yellow line."

"The Capitol was invaded in the morning by folks with only milk in their stomachs. Imagine what would happen if guys coming from a bar, with fire in their bellies, came this way?" He handed her a CSO—crime scene overall, still in its plastic wrapper.

"Oh, thank you," Vikki said. She stepped into it. She placed a hand on his shoulder to steady herself as she put on the booties with one hand. Not an easy fit. "Puff. Thanks again."

He shooed her away with a flick of his wrist. "Go ahead. You have a case waiting."

Vikki left the footpath and walked toward the graves. Her eyes focused on the crime scene, lit with portable standing halogen lamps. Three investigators with CSU vests were crouching, focusing at something of interest. She couldn't believe what she was seeing.

A woman in a black dress, wearing below-the-knee boots with long black hair splayed out around her head, lay on a rectangular, above-ground coffin like grave. She appeared to be gazing at the stars and didn't look more than twenty-five.

Vikki did a double take. She got closer. Were her eyes deceiving her? Dark-reddish, congealed blood ran from the corner of her lip. Black shadows circled her unseeing eyes. Was that a wooden stake jutting out of her chest? She leaned closer.

"Boo!" said a voice behind her.

Vikki yelped and jumped. Adrenaline surged through her body. She whirled to face her tormentor. It was Gomez. She closed her eyes and placed a hand on her chest. Her heart raced like a struck tuning fork "Please don't do that again."

"Sorry. I thought you saw me already," said Gomez. "I think we have a real-life vampire or witch here. Most of all, someone took her out the way they did in medieval Europe by impaling her with a stake."

"Who's the victim?" Vikki asked.

"Caucasian female, maybe in her mid-twenties. She took a spike to the chest—that's about what we know. Her earrings have been ripped off. No phone, no purse, no ID."

Vikki glanced around. If robbery was the motive, that was sad. "Who found her?"

Gomez jerked his head to his left. A man of about fifty-five wearing a thick multicolored sweater, under a dirty blue overall was talking to a uniform.

"What was he doing in the graveyard at the night?" Vikki asked.

"I asked him the same thing," Gomez said. "He's a gravedigger. He said he came searching for his flask and found her." Gomez pointed at a mound. "He said they were hand-digging that and had to call it a night."

"Are graves still dug by hand?"

Gomez beamed. "You ask the same questions I did. Most of the time, they use a backhoe." He looked around. "But, because this area is an older part of the cemetery, probably more than a hundred years old, and the graves dug by hand, the headstones are closer together."

"We have to send uniforms to talk to the businesses around and ask people if they saw or heard anything. Especially CCTV footage of the area."

"It's being done as we speak," Gomez said. He furrowed his forehead as if deep in thought. "Have you seen the ME?"

"Behind you," Vikki said.

Gomez turned. "Ah, Dr. Brandon. I was beginning to wonder what happened to you."

"Hi, Gomez. I had to drop by the morgue to get my tools." He nodded at Vikki. "I don't want to keep your guys waiting." He went closer to the body and did a walk around. Then he brought out his Canon.

Vikki knew the routine. He would take pictures of the victim, catching every detail from two angles. Then he would estimate the time of death through a scientifically proven process. She stepped away to talk to the gravedigger, the mechanical double shutter sound of his camera filling the background.

The ditch-digger's story collaborated with what he'd told Gomez earlier. He'd worked for the cemetery for twenty-five years. Vikki didn't get any whiff of alcohol on his breath.

"Did you find your Thermos?" Vikki asked.

The man raised a medium-sized worn Thermos. "Yes, otherwise the wife won't be happy. And no strong coffee for me tomorrow."

"Mattsen. Gomez. Come over here, please?" It was Dr. Brandon.

"Excuse me," Vikki said and walked over to the ME.

He stood over the vic with a wooden tongue depressor in his hands. "I'm done with the crime scene. Based on temperature and lividity, the time of death was between seven and nine p.m. She's dressed like a vampire, as you can see. And someone drove a spike into her heart."

"That's like a scene out of *Dracula*," Gomez said.

"There's an oily substance on the stake. I'll have the lab analyze it." Dr. Brandon pried the victim's lips open. "See."

Besides the congealed blood by her lip, the victim's teeth were fangs.

CHAPTER THREE

Vikki drove to the PD after the vic was removed from St. Ives Cemetery and taken to the morgue. She'd found no clues. It seemed like someone or something had appeared from nowhere, driven a stake into her heart, and vanished. She remembered the stain on the wooden stake and asked Ted to let her know when he was ready to begin the autopsy.

Vikki was typing out a report when her phone rang. "Mattsen."

"Hey, beautiful."

"Hi," Vikki said. The adrenaline she'd suppressed when they were with other people rushed through her.

"I'm about to begin the autopsy on our Jane Doe. You still want to observe?"

"Sure. I'll be right there." She hung up and turned her computer off. A big smile on Vikki's face was reflected on the monitor. She tried to switch it off, but it refused to go away. Despite all he knew about her, he'd called her beautiful.

Vikki glanced around and considered leaving a message with one of the guys in the office for Gomez. Sean McClane was on the phone. Totally of no help. She wrote on a sticky note and attached it to Gomez's computer.

The ME's office was across the courtyard from the police department. It could also be reached through an underground tunnel. Considering it was already late at night, Vikki took the tunnel.

There was no receptionist at night to delay her. She continued to the autopsy suite, wrinkling her nose as she got closer. It was impossible to get used to the smell of autopsy chemicals and the morgue's constant chilly air.

Ted had laid out a disposable gown, booties, face mask, and hair net in the dressing area. She knew it was for her. She put them on and stepped in.

Vikki nodded and waved at the technician.

He was dressed in a similar outfit as hers. He waved back.

Even though the patients were dead, wearing protective overalls by visitors was to prevent unintentionally contaminating the vic. Especially important in a homicide case.

She walked toward the autopsy table where Ted stood over Jane Doe. Vikki's steps faltered. She'd seen a few cases that had given her pause. But the young woman scrubbed clean of the dark makeup on her face, her clothes removed, looked like she was sleeping rather than dead.

Ted waved her over. "What about Gomez? He's not coming?"

Vikki swallowed and went closer. "He went to the break room to get coffee. I left a note for him."

Ted clasped his gloved hands together. "The forensic tech dusted the spike for fingerprints. Good luck with that. He also swabbed the stick so we could figure out the chemical that was on it. I ordered a rape kit."

Vikki nodded, not wanting to ask the follow-up question.

Ted pointed at her ears, one after the other. "Her earrings were ripped off. And I think the perp took them. The cause of death was manual strangulation." He pointed at the dark coloration around the neck. "Her hyoid bone was broken."

Vikki raised an eyebrow. "Not the spike to the heart?"

Ted nodded. "I'd say she was dressed in a vampire costume—maybe on her way to a costume party. There are many parties going on now." Ted threw out his hand. "This is a guess. Perhaps the perp wanted to throw the investigation off course and make it look like a ritual killing."

Vikki nodded. "Even the way she was displayed on the coffin like a sacrificial offering." She drew in a deep breath and exhaled. "And no ID. No phone. I mean, today, almost every adult carries a cell phone."

"Let's hope the forensic lab will get a match with her fingerprint," Ted said, then growled. "I almost forgot."

"What?" Vikki followed Ted with her eyes.

He walked to a shelf and picked up a sizable clear Ziplock bag. Inside was a black cloth. Vikki came over.

"Her costume. When we removed it, we found this." Ted shook the bag until a tag became visible. "I think it's a consignment store. It has an address, too."

Vikki read out loud, "Authentic Costumes and Storage Units." She let out a deep sigh. 'Finally, a break." She took out her cell and snapped a picture of the tag, then the dress. On a whim, she took a face shot of the victim. She typed the address into her phone's GPS. The store was in Franklin. "They might still be open."

"You're not going to stay for the dissection?" Ted asked.

"Oh no. The spike in the heart is enough excitement for one night. Most of these stores live for Halloween. It doesn't make sense closing early when people are still buying costumes."

The door to the morgue barged open, and Gomez strolled in. "Sorry, I'm late. I got—"

He'd caught sight of the vic on the autopsy table. "My

God. The evil that men do."

Vikki waved the phone in the air. "We have a lead."

CHAPTER FOUR

Vikki drove to the store in Franklin with Gomez riding shotgun. It was almost eleven-thirty when they arrived. To Vikki's surprise, she couldn't find parking. It took two passes before a car pulled out, and Vikki took the space.

Inside the store was like a carnival. A bit dark, but with assorted arrangements of flashing lights, the setup was divided into different sections with displays. Mechanical sounds like grinding gears, roars, talking zombies, laughter, and conversations from shoppers filled the air.

There was a royalty theme section, witches and wizards, pirates, Disney, Harry Potter, superheroes, villains, and many more costume themes Vikki didn't know about.

Vikki chuckled. "This is crazy. All that is missing is popcorn and cotton candy."

Gomez clapped his hands and rubbed them together. "Wow. Costumes galore. I'll check out the arrangement on the right." He took off in a direction with gladiator costumes without waiting for a reply.

Vikki walked around, the odor constantly shifting depending on the section—the smell of fresh rubber from the masks, synthetic hair, and musk. An arrangement of lights around a grotesque clown gave off the stench of heated plastic.

Men, women, and kids roamed the store. If you didn't have a costume in mind before coming in, you were screwed. Deciding on what to get wouldn't be easy. The more Vikki gazed, the more the idea of wearing a costume grew on her.

The accessories were eye-catching, too. The graveyard section had fake tombstones, plastic, life-like rotten hands waiting to be planted in a garden to mimic a zombie about to burst out. And even a machine that pumped mist into the atmosphere.

Vikki passed the slutty section with costumes for nurses, vampires, and princesses. Most of the costumes worn by models on the packaging were tight miniskirts exposing a lot of skin.

She shook her head and smiled when she saw a costume of a female prisoner in a tight, short prison uniform and a policewoman with a tiny blouse and skirt and handcuffs to go with it.

Vikki was at the ghost section when a blood-curdling scream was let loose. The little hairs at the back of her neck rose, and she went for her Glock, stopping short of pulling it out. She gazed around, trying to locate the source.

Nobody seemed panicked. The sound came again, and she noted something mechanical about it—it was a scream machine.

Vikki moved her hand away from her holster, suddenly feeling hot. What she hadn't seen so far was a costume similar to the one the victim was wearing. It was time to talk to an associate.

Vikki noticed a woman with a witch's hat perched on her head. She wore black pants and a black tee shirt with text in yellow that said: *Staff*. Vikki approached her.

"Hello, I'm trying to find a small black vampire dress."

"Aren't we all." She said and smiled. "Over there." She pointed at a vampire section Vikki had already checked out.

Vikki went for her phone in her back pocket. "Hold on. I have a picture."

The staff member leaned forward and examined the picture. She reached for Vikki's screen. "May I?"

"Sure."

The girl tapped the screen, making the image bigger with two fingers. "That tag is from our consignment section." She looked around until she saw what she was searching got "You see the man with gray hair at the customer service desk?"

"Mm-hmm."

"He's Bill. He owns this store, the consignment section, and the next-door storage unit. I'm sure he can help you."

Vikki thanked her and headed to the customer service section. Bill was probably in his sixties, about six feet tall, and was dressed in a butler costume. Two people were in line before her.

Five minutes later, the woman in front of her was almost done with her return. Vikki was tired. She'd go straight to the reason they were there.

"Mattsen," said a familiar voice

Vikki turned to her left.

Gomez walked up with a big smile on his face. "Hey, see what I found? I think it will go well with my gladiator costume. Did you find anything?"

Vikki stared at the giant sword in his hand. "About to."

"Hello, young lady," Bill said in a deep, gravelly voice. "Thanks for your patience. How can I help you?"

Vikki flashed her SIPD badge. "I'm Detective Mattsen, my partner Detective Gomez. I can see it's a busy night. We don't want to take up too much of your time. We're investigating a homicide." She tapped her screen and turned it over to face Bill, not waiting for him to react. "Do you recognize this outfit?"

Bill put on his glasses. He leaned closer to the phone. "I can see the tag. It came from our consignment store. I think I sold it to a cute, smallish—"

Vikki swiped to the left on the screen.

Bill drew back, took a deep breath, and expelled it slowly. "...young lady with black hair."

It was the photo of the vic's face Vikki had taken at the morgue less than an hour ago.

Bill shook his head. "So sorry."

"We're trying to put a name to the face," Gomez said.

Bill wagged a finger in the air. "I think she was here two days ago. I can look up the transaction. The tag is enough." He typed on the computer.

Vikki brushed off invisible lint from her jacket and pulled on the lapel. Were they going to get a break? She couldn't keep still. She watched Bill, waiting for good news.

"There it is. Cindy Kent. Eighteen Bent Lane, St. Ives."

Vikki typed it directly into her phone's GPS.

"Did she come alone?" Gomez asked.

"I'm not so sure," Bill said. "Two other girls were close by when I rang her up. Maybe one of them was with her. This was at the consignment store next door." He looked over Vikki's shoulder.

Vikki turned and noticed that a line had built up behind her. "Thanks so much. We'll come back if we need more info."

"Should we go to the address now?" Gomez asked. "We can do it tomorrow."

Vikki felt energized and said, "Why not. It's close by, and you found something. Maybe you'll find something else there, too."

Gomez chuckled. "Touché."

CHAPTER FIVE

Cindy Kent lived in a two-story apartment unit on Eighteen Bent Lane in St. Ives. It took about fifteen minutes to get there from the costume shop. All through the drive, Gomez admired his new plastic toy, extolling its virtues.

"It seems so realistic," Gomez said. "The gladius." He ran his hand along the flat surface of the sword. "It's similar to the one used by Russel Crowe in the movie *Gladiator*." He turned to Vikki. "Do you know what the word gladiator means?"

Vikki shrugged. "Someone who uses a gladius."

Gomez nodded. "A swordsman. The Roman army was something to behold."

Vikki parked the car along the curb. "Indeed." She opened the door. "I hope you're not bringing your knife?"

"I'm not. And it's a sword."

Vikki pulled her jacket tighter around her to ward off the chill. The street was eerily quiet, like something was about to happen. She raised her head to a low humming sound. The sky was cloudless, punctuated by the blinking lights of a passing aircraft.

Vikki scrutinized the two-story building. The apartments were dark but for the security lights. The main entrance was a few feet from the sidewalk. She walked over and tried the door. It was locked. She checked the time on her phone. It was after twelve. Vikki turned to Gomez. "What do we do?"

"Ring the bell. Maybe the landlord lives in the building?"

Vikki did. By the third ring, lights came on in the ground-floor apartment. About two minutes later, a middle-aged woman wearing a red velvet robe and her blonde hair covered with a net opened the inner door and eyed them with disdain.

Vikki placed her badge against the glass door.

The woman checked out Gomez, who also had his shield against the door. She opened it.

"Detectives, how can I help you at this ungodly hour?" asked the woman. Her voice was thick with sleep.

Vikki turned to Gomez, deferring to him. The woman had focused on him before opening the door.

"Sorry to bother you, I'm Detective Gomez. My partner, Detective Mattsen. Cindy Kent lives here, right?"

The woman's eyes flickered with recognition. "Yes. I'm her landlady. I don't think she's home."

Gomez pursed his lips. "I know."

The woman's eyes narrowed. "So..."

"I'm so sorry to be the bearer of bad news," Gomez said, "but her body was discovered earlier in the evening at the cemetery. Cindy's dead."

The landlady gasped. Blood drained from her face. She was wide awake. "What happened?"

"That's what we're trying to find out," Vikki said. "We'd like to see her apartment. See if we can glean any clues from it."

"My God," the landlady said, her hand going to her neck, staring at the floor. She glanced up. "Don't you need a warrant for that?"

Gomez threw out his hands and shrugged. "We can get one and return later in the morning. But that would only delay us figuring out what happened and arresting who did this."

"Okay, come on." She took them up the stairs to the first floor. She reached into the pocket of her robe and brought out a bunch of keys, her hands shaking. She knocked three times. "Hello, this is the landlady."

There was no reply.

She knocked again. This time she didn't wait for a reply. "If there's anybody there, I'm coming in with the police."

She unlocked the door, and they stepped in.

It was a small space the renter could split into a sitting room, and dining and kitchen. Cindy had a desk in the center of the room. On it was the latest issue of *Vampyre* magazine and a pharmacology textbook.

The bedroom had a bed and a table. One side of the bed had been slept on. There were clothes on the floor. A table with a handheld mirror, makeup tray, and brush was pushed against a wall.

"She is—was—a student at the community college," said the landlady. "Studying to become a pharmacy technician. Most of my renters are students. It's a revolving door, kind of. One student graduates and tells the next about the apartment."

"The bathroom is clear," Gomez said. "This is what I call a student's lair—sparse furnishing. This is about the cleanest I've seen."

"Does she have family close by?" Vikki asked.

The landlady shook her head. "Not that I know of."

"What about a boyfriend?" Gomez asked.

The landlady dabbed her eyes with her knuckle. "She doesn't spend too much time here. She's here mostly to sleep. I hear her more than I see her. We don't have a common room. I only see her if we're outside our rooms simultaneously or in the laundry. In the eight months she was here, it was always a female she came home with. They're laughing and giggling—you know how girls are."

Gomez nodded. She had his full attention.

"A few days ago, she came back with a guy. I know because I heard them arguing. Their voices were short and clipped."

"Arguing about what?" Vikki asked.

"I couldn't make it out."

"Can you describe him?" Gomez asked.

Vikki thought it was a redundant question. She already said she'd only heard her.

The landlady massaged her neck. "A door slammed, followed by footsteps down the stairs. I saw him through the window. A tall man with black hair. He dressed like her."

Vikki narrowed her eyes. "What do you mean? Dressed like her?"

"Whenever I see her, she always wears black, dark makeup." The landlady pointed. "Like the women in that vampire magazine on the table. Maybe she's a Devil worshipper. I don't know."

"Ah, Gothic—the macabre," Gomez said, nodding.

Vikki fished in her pocket. "Do you know anyone who would want to hurt her?"

"I don't know," the landlady said, her voice cracking. Tears rolled down her cheeks. She sniffed and wiped them with the back of her hand. "Maybe check at Mike's Diner where she worked. It's close to the cemetery at the end of the street."

Vikki gave her a card and thanked her. "Call me if you remember anything or just to talk." She resisted the urge to tell her Cindy had been found with a wooden stake through her heart.

Once inside the car, Gomez said, "You can drop me off at the PD so I can pick up my car."

CHAPTER SIX

Vikki was in the squad room by nine a.m. She wore navy-blue pants, a black blouse, and a suede jacket. She'd brought her black peacoat, which she hung on the back of her chair.

The office was a more cheerful place since McClane had toned down his rhetoric. Detective Sean McClane, her nemesis from her rookie days in New York, had stopped harassing her for unknown reasons.

She'd kneed him in the groin when he'd touched her inappropriately back then, and he'd ended up with emergency surgery. Since then, he'd harassed her at every opportunity, but that had ended abruptly. Maybe someone higher up had talked to him.

Vikki took a sip of her coffee and thought of the previous night. She'd gone home since Ted was at the morgue completing the autopsy on Cindy Kent.

Exhausted, she'd showered, changed, and crashed.

She'd slept straight through the night. A feat she rarely accomplished these days.

Vikki turned her computer on and was about to look up Mike's Diner when Gomez walked in. He wore a black suit and had a coffee mug from home, too. The writing was on the wall—they had a lot to do.

Gomez smiled at her. "Good morning, Detective. I hope you slept well. I tried on my complete Halloween costume last night. The sword is perfect. Even Serena agreed."

Vikki wanted to say: Serena didn't want to argue with you at two a.m. Instead, she said, "I can't wait to see the complete ensemble."

Gomez sat and pushed the "on" switch for his computer. As it booted, he said, "Did you do any research on the diner where Cindy worked?"

Before she could answer, the phone on Vikki's table rang. "Mattsen."

"Good morning. Can I see you and Gomez in my office?"

"Yes, sir."

The captain had already hung up.

Gomez raised an eyebrow. "Captain Levin?"

Vikki got up. "Yep. He wants us in his office." She picked up her mug, took a sip, and headed for the office.

Gomez was right behind her.

Captain Levin sat in front of the window, his favorite spot with a view of the courtyard. About six feet, six inches tall, lean, and wearing his customary navy-blue suit, he could be posing for a photo.

Captain Levin turned slowly to face them, arms clasped behind his back. "Any news on the murder in the cemetery last night? We cannot have a killer on the loose on Halloween week."

Vikki brought him up to speed with what they'd done the previous night and their plans for this morning. "It's a bit bizarre, I must say. The young woman was dressed as a vampire. She wore all black. Had fangs in her mouth, like a modern-day vampire. Someone strangled her and put a stake through her heart."

Captain Levin gave her an incredulous stare. "Like what they did to Christopher Lee in *Dracula*? But..." The captain hesitated. "Any reason to believe she was a...vampire?"

Gomez shook his head. "Her apartment didn't yield anything of the occult. She seems to be a girl who enjoyed dressing in black clothing and wearing dark makeup."

"But someone believed otherwise," Captain Levi said. "They strangled her first, then drove a spike into her chest."

"Either the work of a believer or someone trying to push us in a different direction," Vikki said. "We hope to learn more when we talk to the people where she worked."

The captain stood and walked toward his chair. The signal that the meeting was over. He let out a breath. "In addition to this homicide, there's the problem of drug peddlers passing off colored fentanyl as candy, hoping to create a new market. The mayor doesn't want to be remembered as being in office when Halloween or trick or treat was canceled in St. Ives."

Vikki had heard about Rainbow Fentanyl. That wouldn't be a new market. They'd be creating a new generation of parents who lost a child before their child celebrated their tenth birthday.

"Vikki, a penny for your thoughts," Captain Levin said.

"I heard about the New Jersey woman arrested in Manhattan with thousands of colored fentanyl pills in Lego boxes." She shook her head. "Imagine a kid getting hold of that thinking it was Skittles?" A shudder went through her as she spoke. "That will devastate the community. If Halloween must be canceled, the mayor has to 'mayor up' and do whatever is needed."

The captain brushed off imaginary lint from his suit. "I hear you, Detective. That was the only issue I had until this Halloween-themed homicide came up, too. Now go find out who's responsible for this."

Vikki nodded. "Yes, sir."

"Gomez," Captain Levin said. "Attendance to your costume...s-s—"

"Soirée, sir," Vikki said.

"Whatever, Mattsen! We know you speak French. Gomez, the attendance to that—greatly depends on the outcome of this investigation."

CHAPTER SEVEN

Vikki and Gomez walked into Mike's Diner, a fifties-themed restaurant on the same street as the cemetery. There was no way you could see it from where she'd parked the previous night. It was probably a ten-minute walk, but you could smell it if the winds were right.

Inside, it had all the bells and whistles—stainless-steel trimmings, a jukebox, a life-size cutout of Fat Elvis, and a mouthwatering menu: cheeseburgers, mashed potatoes, bacon, meatloaf, eggs, sausages, giant stacks of golden pancakes—traditional American comfort food.

Vikki's stomach rumbled. The smell of bacon, fried eggs, and toast hung in the air. She was tempted to order.

Gomez licked his lips and swallowed several times, his gaze glued to the menu. She'd take her cue from him.

There were about six people in the restaurant. The sound of conversations, cutlery on ceramic, and sizzling from the kitchen filled the air.

A couple sat in the booth on their left. Businesspeople out for breakfast, Vikki thought.

"Waiter, where's our coffee?" the woman said.

"It's coming. Sorry, we're a bit short-staffed this morning," said a middle-aged man wearing an apron that said Mike's Diner.

Vikki and Gomez stood in line. A man with blond hair, a thick beard, and broad shoulders sat in a corner. He looked strong and could pass for a Viking. A plate of pancakes, hash browns, bacon, and sunny-side-up eggs was in front of him. Fork in hand, he stared at his food, but it seemed his mind was far away.

Then it was Vikki's turn. She refocused her gaze on the person behind the counter.

"What can I get you?" the cashier asked in a sassy voice. All that was missing was chewing gum.

Vikki flashed her shield. "I'm Detective Mattsen with SIPD. My colleague, Detective Gomez. We have a few questions about Cindy Kent."

The cashier's eyes drifted to the middle-aged man wearing an apron, then back to Vikki. "She was supposed to be here... but she's not."

"That's right!" the apron-clad man said gruffly. He dropped what he was doing and came closer. "You said Cindy Kent?"

Vikki stepped out of the line. "Yes." She took a few steps to the side. "Good morning. And who are you?"

He placed both hands on his waist. A smile that said, 'Are you seriously asking who I am?' split his lips. "Mike Stanley, owner and manager."

Okay, Vikki thought—an egocentric owner.

"Can I be of service to you?" Mike asked. His voice was quieter.

That's better, thought Vikki. *At least he's rational. Won't cause an uproar in front of his customers and potential customers and let his emotions drag his business down.*

"Detective Victoria Mattsen, SIPD. I have a few questions to ask—"

Mike raised a hand. "I don't know what's wrong with young kids today. You employ them, give them a chance. They come in and go into a trance while they're supposed to be working. Nobody wants to work."

"When was the last time you saw her?" Vikki asked.

"Yesterday around six, an hour before her shift was over," Mike said, anger creeping into his voice again. "I had a million and one people in here, and she left. Put on a costume like she was Elvira, her eyes and lips painted black, and left. If you see her, tell her not to bother coming back."

"Mike...Mike!" It was the man who had been staring at his food.

Vikki glanced at his plate. He hadn't eaten much, but the pancakes now looked like Pacman.

The diner owner whirled. "Mel, come on. I know she's your favorite waitress. She left early yesterday." He pointed at the wall clock. "She's still not here."

Mel raised his hand and extended his forefinger and thumb, mimicking a phone. "Did you call her?" His voice was gruff and deep.

"I'm the employer here, Mel," Mike said, the tips of both hands on his chest. "She should be calling me and letting me know if she's taking a sick day or running late."

Mel poured syrup on his pancakes and started to eat with vigor. "Well, if you let her go, I'll stop eating here. Fair is fair."

Mike studied him. He opened his mouth, then closed it.

Vikki felt it was time for her to step in and defuse the situation before it escalated. Who was this guy who had had the owner of the diner tongue-tied? Where was Gomez? She glanced over her shoulder. He pointed at the picture menu behind the cashier, ensuring she got his order right.

Vikki turned to the man, Mel. "Sir." She gave him a nod. "If you don't mind, sir, I need to speak with Mike."

"Be my guest," Mel said with a wave.

Vikki turned to the owner. "Is there a place we can talk in private?"

Mike nodded. "Sure, my office. Come on." He walked toward the back.

Vikki followed.

He entered an office big enough for a desk chair and metal cabinet. Mike crossed his arms over his stomach. "Okay, go ahead." His voice was low.

"Last night, Cindy Kent's body was discovered in the cemetery."

Mike Stanley stared at her as if there was more. "Okay, when is she coming back?"

"Cindy Kent won't be coming back at all—she's dead."

"What do you mean she's dead?" Mike said, his voice rising. "I saw her walk out of here by six p.m. last night. We're short of staff. I need her here. When is she coming back?"

Vikki cocked her head and pursed her lips. The man was dead serious. "Mr. Stanley, Cindy Kent was murdered last night."

The word murder must have done the trick. Blood drained from Mike's face. He leaned back and sat on the edge of the desk.

"She was killed?" His voice was barely a whisper. "My God."

Vikki gave him time to recover. She had follow-up questions.

"What happened?" asked Mike, clearly trying not to choke on his words, his head clasped between his palms.

"We're still investigating. Her body was found in the cemetery around eight."

Mike's head jerked up. His bloodshot eyes bore into Vikki's. "I heard the police sirens. It was in response to her?"

"Mattsen. Everything all right?" Gomez asked behind Vikki.

"Yes, we're almost done. Mr. Stanley, where were you between seven and nine?" Vikki already knew the answer.

"I was right here, drowning in orders. Any of my staff and customers can verify that." He shook his head. "And...and she was fighting for her life. Despite my ranting earlier, I liked her a lot. I wanted her to succeed..."

"Mr. Stanley, do you know anyone who could have done this?" Gomez asked.

"I don't know...ask her boyfriend. He's in a band, Ghosts or Ghouls. I think his name is Brian or Davis. I overheard her on the phone arguing with him." He shrugged. "Maybe the argument was nothing."

Vikki gave him her card.

CHAPTER EIGHT

They left Mike's Diner with two paper bags of to-go food containers. Gomez had ordered food while Vikki had been talking to Mike Stanley.

Vikki turned into New Cemetery Road. "You said the Mel guy left after I went to the back with Mr. Stanley?"

"Yes. They brought him a brown paper takeaway bag like this one. Gomez touched the bag the food came in and sighed. "I wonder what else they will ban in New Jersey." He stabbed a piece of pancake, egg, and sausage with his fork and shoveled them into his mouth.

Vikki's mind was still on Mel. "Maybe there was someone at home he bought food for?"

"Out of curiosity, I asked the cashier about him. She said he was a regular and always bought extra food." Gomez nodded. "You could be right. But he and the owner seem to go back a long way."

Back at the police station, Gomez, stuffed from eating in the car, went to his desk to get a head start on their new lead from Mike Stanley.

"What you can't find on Google isn't worth knowing," she'd said.

Vikki headed to the breakroom to eat her food. The room was empty, a rarity. And almost quiet, too, but for the vending machine and refrigerator hum. Someone, perhaps Jody, the police department's admin secretary, had done a little Halloween decorating.

A zombie butler, about five feet tall, dressed in rags, with an eyeball hanging by a thread from its socket, stood close to the vending machine holding out a tray with candy.

Vikki put the last bite of pancake in her mouth and wondered what four-letter word Gomez was muttering under his breath as he searched for Ghost, Ghoul, Brian, and Davis.

"Are you going to Detective Gomez's costume party?" a familiar voice asked.

Vikki cocked her head. It was Maria Santiago, a new detective whom Vikki liked. She smiled. "I'd planned to until we got this vampire case last night."

"I heard. I was going to go as a vampire," Santiago said. "I hope you solve it soon, so Halloween won't be toned down or canceled."

"I hope so, too."

Santiago walked to the vending machine, inserted coins into the slot, and pushed a button. A bottle of water tumbled down, and she retrieved it. "See you around."

Vikki waved and watched her disappear through the door. She packed the empty food container and put it in the garbage, then headed upstairs to see how Gomez was doing.

Vikki flopped into her seat in the detective squad room next to Gomez's desk.

"Did you wolf the food down?" Gomez asked. He waved a dismissive hand. "That's good you ate fast. I think I found something." He turned his monitor toward Vikki. "The boyfriend. Mr. Stanley wasn't too far off from the names he dropped."

Vikki didn't know what to make of the website. It looked like something out of a horror movie. It belonged to a music group called Ghost. Cindy Kent's landlady was right. The band was an excellent example of birds of the same feather flocking together. The band members were all dressed in black with dark makeup.

"His name is Brian Davis, and he runs Ghouls' Coven."

"What's that?"

Gomez chuckled. "A place where like-minded people come together to interact. I also searched them on Facebook." He clicked on another tab, and the Ghost page on the social media site popped up. He tapped on a photo. "Check this out."

It was a picture of Brian Davis with a tall, beautiful girl beaming from ear to ear, standing beside him. It was the victim during happier times. Was he responsible for what had happened to her?

Vikki woke her phone with a tap. "It's about ten-thirty a.m. Let's visit Brian Davis and see if he can shine some light on this investigation."

CHAPTER NINE

To get to the street, they'd passed through a one-way tunnel blasted through a hill in the days when St. Ives and most of Sussex County had been a booming mining district. It was as beautiful as it was eerie.

It was in an older part of town with mostly artisan shops. An antique furniture store was next door. On the other side stood a house with a wooden water wheel attached. The creek that supplied the water was still there, as it had probably been more than a hundred years ago, but not connected to turn the wheel.

Vikki stopped in front of the house with the address for Ghouls' Coven. She got out of the car and inhaled the clean, cold air. The sun was up and shining brightly, but it was chilly. Vikki put on her peacoat and approached the door.

"I should have brought a jacket," Gomez said, rubbing his palms together.

The front lawn had tombstones strewn across it. Vikki couldn't tell if they were props or if the house was in an actual graveyard. Some of the props were obvious—like hands sticking out of the ground and a half-buried coffin showing a skeleton.

At the door, Vikki reached for the knocker and hesitated. It was a human skull made of metal. "Nice." She knocked three times and listened for approaching footsteps.

Nothing.

Vikki banged on the door with the heel of her hand.

Gomez cocked his head, ear toward the door. "I think someone's home."

Moments later, the door opened, and a man, probably in his late twenties, wearing a black robe, poked out his head. He shielded his eyes from the sun.

Vikki raised her badge. "SIPD. Is Brian Davis here?"

"Brian?" said the man.

Vikki held her breath after she got the first whiff of dragon breath. Luckily for her, the man stepped back and waved them in.

"Please shut the door behind you. It's cold," he said and tightened the robe. He walked through a door and pointed. "Brian is sleeping over there."

The room was dark, lit by a flickering old-school lantern with yellow flames. Vikki was sure they had velvet curtains or something heavy that blotted out the light completely.

"What the fuck?" Gomez said. "You're shitting me."

Gomez never threw four-letter words around for the fun of it. Vikki had to see. What was there sent shivers down her spine. It was a half-open coffin with a man's torso showing. He lay with his palms resting on his chest.

"Is he dead?" Gomez asked and leaned forward.

The man's eyes shot open.

Vikki backed away. "What the...?"

The man yawned, stretched, and climbed out of the coffin. He was dressed all in black.

"Sorry for the theatrics." He pointed at a CCTV monitor

screen. "I saw you coming and couldn't help myself. "I'm Brian Davis. You can call me Brian. Did you say you're the police?"

"We are the police. If you know what's good for you, don't pull that stunt on us again!" Gomez said. A hand was placed on his chest. "I almost had a heart attack."

"My apologies again. I run a haunted house, and it's difficult to find people completely unexpectant."

Gomez flipped his jacket to the side and showed his holstered Glock. "You see, I watch the living dead, too, and the only way to put them down for good is by deadly force. And the department will back me up."

Vikki clasped her hands. "Okay, Brian, can we get more light here, for starters?"

"Sure." He picked up a remote control, and the flickering lantern stopped and changed to bright-white light.

"Better," Vikki said. She watched Brian as she spoke. "We're here about Cindy Kent."

Brian's face tightened. He leaned against the closed section of his coffin. "What about her?"

"When was the last time you saw her?" Vikki asked.

"A couple of days ago, at her apartment."

Vikki nodded. "A credible source said they heard loud voices coming from her apartment and later saw someone matching your description leaving. What were you arguing about?"

Brain held out his hands, palm out. "Wow, wow. Hold your horses. What's going on? Did something happen?"

"You tell us," Gomez said and came closer to Brian.

Brian's nose flared. Vikki expected him to ask if he'd committed an offense or ask for a lawyer.

"She wanted us to break up and explore other relationships. I stormed off after that. Later, after I'd simmered down, I thought about it. Maybe it was a good thing. You know what they say about releasing what you love. If it comes back, it's yours for keeps."

Vikki wanted to say, set it free, and it's bye-bye forever, but she kept her mouth shut. "Okay."

"I decided to do that, and we agreed to meet here by seven p.m., but she never made it. I called her several times—I haven't heard from her. It goes straight to voice mail."

Vikki inhaled and let out a sigh. "Do you know who she might have wanted to explore a relationship with?"

Brian had a silly grin on his face. "She's always hanging out with one particular girl, so I hoped that would benefit me, too, in the long run."

Gomez seemed to have had enough. He still looked pissed from the casket joke. Shaking his head, he stabbed a finger in front of Brian. "That's not what happened. You knew she was going to leave you no matter what, and you waited in the cemetery. And when she came along, you attacked her and strangled her." Gomez nodded. "You set her free, all right. Now no one else can have her."

Brian sprang to his feet. "What! Cindy's dead?"

Vikki nodded. "I'm so sorry." Her voice was whispery, apologetic. "Where were you between seven and nine p.m. on Tuesday?"

"I was right here—waiting for Cindy. I love her. Her happiness is my concern. That's why I agreed to set her free."

"Did anyone see you?"

"It was a party. We caught it all on video."

Vikki sighed. "I'll like to see the clips." She watched as tears cascaded down Brian's face. "Do you know anyone who would have wanted to hurt her?"

Brian shook his head.

"What's the name of the girl she was involved with?" Gomez asked.

Brian glared at him. "I can't remember her name now."

"Maybe you'll come with us to the station. That should help your memory."

"Hazel, Hazel Wheeler," Brian said.

Gomez gave him his card. "Do you know where we can find her?"

"No."

"Call if you remember anything more, and please don't leave town without checking with us."

CHAPTER TEN

Vikki and Gomez were back at the office by eleven a.m. It was a quiet drive back from the haunted house.

Gomez had been a bit aggressive with Brian Davis. What Davis had done was stupid, but to give him the benefit of the doubt, he hadn't known they were cops and armed. Vikki let it go for now. She didn't want to let her emotions get the better of her and kept quiet rather than trying to talk to Gomez and it didn't come out right.

Vikki picked up a note on her desk. "This is the part of the job I dread."

"Which part?" Gomez asked while doing a one-finger alphabet fishing expedition on his keyboard as he typed.

"Speaking to the next of kin."

"We can go together if you want," Gomez said. "I don't like it either." He looked up. "Didn't we see the beauty queen's family together? And here we are, planning another one."

Vikki nodded. "We don't need to go. One of the uniforms went already. He left a note."

Gomez took a deep breath and sighed. "I think I overdid it with Brian. I was freaked out and pissed off when he pulled the living dead stunt. What if I'd shot him? Then I'd have that on my conscience."

She was glad he'd brought it up. "I panicked, too. He wouldn't have done that if he knew we were packing." Vikki tapped a finger against her lips, deep in thought. "I wonder what makes people do stupid things that could lead to unintended consequences?"

"Like what?"

"You know, wearing all black, sleeping in a coffin, piercings, tatts, drawing attention to oneself unnecessarily."

"I can tell you peer pressure is a big one," Gomez said. "Then there's the other spectrum where abused kids grow up trying to save others from being abused like they were." He shrugged. "Some of them grow up to join groups where they feel at home, like wear black, or join cults, while others join the Army or become cops."

Vikki felt like she'd been struck with a sledgehammer. She'd never told anybody everything about her childhood. Not even Captain Levin. She'd only told Ted about her love life, not her childhood. And nothing to Gomez. Was that why she'd easily been convinced to become a cop? To protect others from what she'd been through?

She heard her name and a phone ringing in the distance.

"Mattsen, are you going to get that?"

His words pulled her out of her reverie. She refocused on Gomez. "What?"

He pointed. "The phone. Are you okay?"

Vikki realized her phone was ringing. "Oh. Sorry. My mind was far away." She picked it up. "Detective Mattsen."

"Who was that?" Gomez asked after she hung up.

"Our vics mother. "They are anxious for more detail about

know what happened to their daughter. They are on their way here."

"What?"

"They were adamant...and I didn't know what to do, considering they had lost a child."

CHAPTER ELEVEN

"I'm so sorry for your loss," Vikki said to Mr. And Mrs. Kent and their other daughter, Kim.

They sat on a couch in Captain Levin's office, unaware of the challenges Vikki had gone through to secure them a room. Her last resort had been the interview rooms, but both had been occupied.

The captain had gracefully offered his office to her when he'd seen her running around like a chicken with its head chopped off. He was famished and had decided to get his lunch at that time.

"When was the last time you saw Cindy?" Vikki asked.

She and Gomez sat on sofas opposite them.

Mrs. Kent dabbed her eyes with a tissue. "About four weeks ago. She always said school and work were demanding. That was why she couldn't visit more."

Mr. Kent's eyes were moist. He seemed to want to speak but hadn't gotten there yet. Kim was the only dry eye amongst them.

"Is there anyone you think who would have wanted to hurt her?" Gomez asked.

Mr. Kent shook his head. "Not the friends we knew from when she lived at home. We didn't know her new friends—the ones she dressed up like."

"Had she ever brought them to the house?" Vikki asked.

"Sometimes they'd drive her in their car," Mr. Kent said, twiddling his thumbs.

Vikki clasped her hands together in front of her. She felt their pain. "When did this transition to dressing up all in black start?" Her voice was low and sounded agonized.

Mrs. Kent sniffled. "I can't say for sure."

"It was gradual," Mr. Kent said. "Maybe by twelfth grade. It was only when she started with dark eyeshadows, lipsticks, and going for a Gothic theme that we noticed."

"Apart from her new friends, are there any friends from high school who dress like her who she keeps in touch with? Any boyfriends, old or current?"

Both parents shook their heads. Kim looked like she had something to say. Vikki was about to ask her what was on her mind when Mr. Kent spoke.

"What about your investigations?" His chin was raised. There was a tightness in his eyes that wasn't there moments ago. "What have you uncovered so far?"

Vikki knew about grief and its different stages. The question seemed to come from nowhere. He was lashing out. She had gone through them several times. As a child, when she hadn't understood what was going on, and as a grown woman, when she had an idea. It was never something you got used to.

The griever tries to process and adjust to their new reality. They go through denial, anger, bargaining, depression, and finally, acceptance. The Kents weren't close yet.

Since she'd got the call last night, she'd been chasing leads with Gomez. But Mr. Kent didn't know that. Vikki steeled herself not to let her emotions take over—amygdala hijack. Like what had happened to Gomez with Brian.

"We are retracing her steps as best as we can," Vikki said. "We are also awaiting lab results that will guide us. Right now, robbery seems to be the motive. Her phone, purse, jewelry, were all taken."

Mrs. Kent let out a sob. "Jewelry? Those dark plastic things got her in trouble?"

Her husband wrapped his hand around her shoulder. "I think we should go now and let you do your job," Mr. Kent said. He stood and helped his wife up.

Vikki felt the tension leave her like someone sitting on her shoulder had jumped off. "This is my card. If you want to talk or have information you want to share, please call me at any time."

Vikki walked with them to the exit, then headed back. She was waiting for the elevator when Mrs. Kent came up alone.

"Detective Mattsen."

"Mrs. Kent, did you forget something?"

She shook her head. "I didn't want to say this in front of Kim. When Cindy was seven, she was sexually abused by a babysitter. We came home one day early and caught them in bed, naked. We fired her, but this had probably been going on for a long time. She was our neighbor's daughter, and we always used her whenever my husband and I had a date night." She paused. "I-I thought you should know as you investigate."

Vikki thanked her, and Mrs. Kent left to rejoin her family. Vikki made a mental note to somehow connect with Kim Kent. She went back to her desk.

Gomez, sitting at his desk next to her, looked up from his computer. "They left?"

Vikki took a deep breath and let it out noisily through her nose. She nodded, then told him about the abuse.

Gomez tapped a finger on his desk. "Growing up, Cindy must have always questioned her sexual orientation. Was Brian right?"

Vikki's desk phone rang. "Mattsen."

The caller was from forensics. "The prints lifted from the wooden stake were good. We ran it through the DMV. We have a match."

CHAPTER TWELVE

Vikki hung up and sat on her chair.

"Who was that?" Gomez asked.

"Forensics. They have a match. The fingerprints lifted from the stake. There were a few partials, but one was complete. Hazel Wheeler."

Gomez muttered the name a few times. "Hazel Wheeler. Isn't that the name Brian Davis gave us? The girl Cindy was leaving him for?"

Vikki nodded, remembering what the landlady had said. 'In the eight months she was here, it was only a female she brought back. They're laughing and giggling—you know how girls are.'

"She's already in the system," Vikki said. "We have to find her."

"I'm on it," said Gomez and faced his monitor. As he typed, he said, "Maybe the mayor won't have to cancel Halloween after all."

Vikki also went on her computer. Her fingers were poised over the keyboard, ready to strike, while her mind was elsewhere. What had possessed Hazel to murder Cindy? They were supposed to be good friends.

"I have the address!" Gomez said.

Vikki got up and removed her peacoat from the back of her chair. "We'd better get going."

Gomez powered off his computer. "What if she's not there?"

"Until we get to that fork in the road..."

CHAPTER THIRTEEN

Vikki and Gomez arrived at twenty-eight Marple Street by two p.m., a twenty-minute drive from the PD. Hazel Wheeler's apartment was in a two-story building, walking distance from Cindy's apartment.

A moving van was parked close to the handicapped spot with its rear door open. Someone was either moving in or moving out, thought Vikki. The main entrance into the apartment was propped open with a stone. And there was nobody in sight. They walked in.

The faint odor of garbage and new carpet hung in the air. Vikki associated that smell with new apartment complexes or those that got a do-over. But that unique smell combination never went away.

The small, carpeted lobby with white walls had mailboxes against one side. Next to the mailboxes was a shut door.

Vikki pointed at the door. "Gomez, you think that's the apartment manager's office?"

"Could be. Based on the size, maybe a utility room, too. But he's probably not here."

Vikki noticed a piece of paper on the floor and walked over. "There's a note. It says: Will be back soon."

Gomez came over. "They must have camera's around to keep an eye on things. Yep, there's one behind you, top right."

Vikki turned. It was an emergency light with two bulbs

Gomez waved at the camera. "Smile, you're on Candid Camera."

"Second floor," Vikki said, glancing at a diagram on the wall. She took the stairs to the second floor. Room twenty-eight was at the end of the corridor.

They hadn't met anybody, but someone was around from the faint sound of a TV somewhere in the building. Vikki knocked on the door and waited.

There was no response.

"You think she's in school?" Gomez asked.

Vikki shrugged and banged on the door again. "Hazel Wheeler, this is the police. Open the door!" There was still no response. She knocked two more times. "I guess we'll have to kick it in. We have probable cause. Her fingerprint on the murder weapon." Vikki took a step back.

"Hold on!"

Vikki stopped. "What? You think I can't kick it down?"

Gomez reached into the pocket and brought out a lock pick gun. "This way we don't have to worry about putting it back together." He raised it and admired it.

"You came prepared."

Gomez inserted the pin into the keyhole. He pulled the trigger once, twice, there was a click, and the door unlocked.

Vikki took out her Glock and stepped in.

The apartment was quiet but for the humming of the refrigerator. "Anybody home? This is the police. Come out with your hands up." They were met with silence.

She caught Gomez's eyes and indicated she'd check out

the bedroom. In less than two minutes, they'd secured the apartment. Nobody was home.

Vikki holstered her Glock. The bedroom only had a bed, a table, and a chair. The apartment's arrangement was similar to Cindy's. She slipped on a pair of latex gloves and picked up a picture of Cindy and Hazel on the nightstand. She flipped it over. There was nothing written on it.

The bed was made. Did that mean she hadn't slept on it last night? Or she had and made the bed before leaving?

Vikki rifled through the papers and magazines on a table in the bedroom. "You think she skipped town?" she asked.

"I don't know! I'm still processing the whole thing. It doesn't make sense. If she did kill her friend, what's her motive? Jealousy? Maybe she didn't know about the coming separation from Brian Davis?"

Vikki chuckled. "Maybe it's a case of if I can't have him, then nobody else can." She heard the sound of the fridge opening.

"No. The murder was brutal. Strangling someone is not easy. Driving a stake through their skin and into their heart is no walk in the park either. Unless she had help. But still, the why?"

Vikki found a receipt from the costume store for a black dress and another from the consignment section for a mystery bag. They already knew about that. She took a picture of each one with her phone and put both receipts in an evidence bag.

She looked back at the table and froze. "What the…?" Vikki moved the magazine to the side. "Gomez, come and see this."

CHAPTER FOURTEEN

"Okay, let me see if I'm following," said Captain Levin.

Vikki and Gomez had gone for a late lunch at the tavern close to the station. They were about to leave when Captain Levin had come in and joined them. She'd thanked him for making his office available at such short notice. She'd debriefed him on the latest development.

"So, Hazel Wheeler's fingerprints were found on the wooden stake recovered from the victim. And you recovered a second wooden stake from her apartment."

Gomez nodded.

"And Mallory and his people are trying to lift fingerprints from it."

"Yes," Vikki said. "We rush the processing to compare it to Hazel Wheeler's once it's ready."

"So where is Hazel Wheeler right now?" Captain Levin asked.

Vikki pursed her lips. She realized they'd dropped the ball. Finding Hazel was the number one priority. But they'd only got sidetracked because she hadn't been there and they'd found something else.

Gomez sighed and said, "We'd hoped to find her in the apartment, but she wasn't there. Instead, we found another wooden stake. So now we're getting it processed."

Captain Levin got up. "I have to order my food. You'd better issue a BOLO. Her fingerprints must be on the spike." He shrugged. "It was found in her apartment. Maybe there might be other prints. But she holds the key to what happened to Cindy Kent and...also whether Halloween would be canceled in St. Ives or not."

Vikki got the message. She sprang to her feet. "Thank you, sir."

They walked back to the PD and to their desks. Gomez peeled away to take care of the BOLO.

Vikki called after him, "Remember to add to be cautious when approaching her. One person is dead, and she seems to have access to a deadly weapon."

She sat at her desk and turned on the computer. She logged in to the database to learn more about Hazel Wheeler. This was like putting the cart before the horse. The only place she showed up was at DMV, which they already had. Her car was a blue 2010 Honda Accord.

She tried Google and ended up on her Facebook page. But only Hazel Wheeler's friends were welcome. Vikki was contemplating her next move when her phone rang.

"Mattsen."

"Hi, forensics here. Hazel Wheeler's prints are on this one. There were no partials. It was all hers."

Vikki thanked them and hung up. It was a repeat of a few hours ago. She must learn more about her. Her place of work, at least, maybe her other friends. Who would have all that information? The school.

Vikki checked the time on her computer: three thirty-nine p.m. She picked up the phone on her desk and called

Sussex Community College. She asked for Ms. Mary Shelley in student affairs.

"The office closes by four p.m.," the receptionist said. "She might have left already. But I'll transfer you."

"Okay." The tone on the line died. Had she hung up? Then it started to ring again. Vikki exhaled. *Please answer* became her mantra for the next few seconds.

"Mary Shelley," said a breathless voice.

"Ms. Shelley, this is Detective Mattsen. I need your help."

"Talk to me."

Vikki told her. In less than five minutes, she had the address of where Hazel Wheeler worked and the phone number. Vikki thanked her and hung up.

Gomez returned with two cups of coffee and handed one over to Vikki. "Freshly made mud. Not what you're used to, but it should do for now."

Vikki took a sip. Sometimes, coffee from the break room was as good as coffee from the best stores if the moment was right. And right now, it could be better.

"Every uniform out there is on the lookout for a blue 2010 Honda Accord and the owner," Gomez said. "Hopefully, we'll get a break soon."

Vikki told him about getting the number for Hazel's place of work. She worked at a massage parlor in Rockaway Mall. "We can follow up with classmates tomorrow." She picked up her office phone. "I'll call and see if she's there." She punched in the number. It was answered on the third ring.

"I'm Detective Victoria Mattsen from St. Ives Police Station. May I speak with Hazel Wheeler, please?"

There was a pause. "Hazel is not here. She was supposed to come in by two p.m."

Vikki's stomach tightened. All she could think of was a worst-case scenario. She'd skipped town. "When was the last time you saw her?"

"One moment, let me check the schedule. I was off sick the last couple of days."

As Vikki waited, she thought of the difference between this lady and Ms. Shelley. Mary Shelley was like a bulldog standing on guard. Their job titles were different.

A beep sounded in Vikki's ear. She looked at the phone. It was an incoming call from the medical examiner's office—Ted. It must be something to do with the case.

"Hello, Detective?" the woman said.

"Yes, I'm here. So she was in on Monday. Off Tuesday... and was supposed to be here now. Is everything okay?"

Now was Vikki's turn not to be forthcoming with information. "We're trying to locate her. Please have her call SPID or call me directly at this number if she shows up." Vikki recited her number, thanked her, and hung up.

Gomez raised an eyebrow. "What did they say?"

"They last saw her on Monday. She was supposed to be there since two p.m. today." She picked up the phone again and punched in some numbers. "The ME called while I was speaking with the woman."

"Good, maybe something came up," Gomez said.

"Ted! Dr. Brandon. Sorry, I was on the phone earlier."

"I was about to call Gomez. Anyway, the rape kit came back. There was no rape...no DNA either. It was expected since there were no external signs of that. But sometimes even consensual helps with figuring out where the vic was earlier and making a connection."

Vikki was quiet. That should be good news, but she was disappointed.

"Are you there?" Ted asked.

"Yes." She laughed. "I was expecting another outcome."

Ted sighed. "I know but cheer up. I'm sure something will come up soon. I have to go. Hopefully, I'll see you tonight." The line went dead.

Vikki put the phone on its cradle and turned to give Gomez the news. He was on the phone.

Gomez held up a finger. His eyes sparkled. "Tell me! Tell me!" His voice got louder. More confident. "About time! Thank you so much, bye."

The excitement he felt was contagious.

Vikki's pulse was racing. "What happened?"

"They found Hazel's car."

CHAPTER FIFTEEN

Vikki couldn't believe what she was hearing. "Hazel's car was found right in her apartment's parking lot?"

"Well, behind it," Gomez said. "If that makes you feel better. Mattsen, we weren't looking for her car when we went there, so let it go."

He was right. But she seemed to be slipping—too many rookie mistakes. Gomez was not catching them—well, his mind was wrapped around his gladius.

They'd pulled up at twenty-eight Marple Street by six-fifteen p.m. A police cruiser was on the scene at the back of the building. Vikki parked next to it.

She stepped out, felt the evening chill, and turned up the collar of her coat. With the sun gone, there was no bright sunlight to deceive the body into thinking it was warm. She shivered and walked toward the officer, talking to a man. She recognized the officer.

"Hi, John."

John Acosta was a new hire. Black hair, broad shoulders, and learning one day at a time. He looked like what Vikki envisioned Gomez at twenty-six.

He nodded at Mattsen and Gomez. "Detectives. This is Jordan, the apartment manager."

Vikki took a step back and let Gomez take the lead.

Gomez scrutinized the redhead with a red beard under the streetlamp's glow. He stood at about five feet nothing.

"Is that a first or last name?" Gomez asked.

Jordan eyed Gomez. "Just, Jordan," he said in a squeaky voice. He cocked his head. He glanced from Gomez to Vikki and back to Gomez. "You kind of look familiar." He took a step back, eyes widening. "You two were at the apartment this morning. The security cameras caught you."

Heat rushed to Vikki's cheeks. The word 'caught' made it sound like something nefarious was going on. "I'm Detective Victoria Mattsen, Detective Gomez is my partner, and we were checking on Hazel Wheeler."

Jordan shook his head. "She wasn't here then and not here now. That's what I told the officer. But that's her car over there." He pointed at the blue vehicle.

Vikki glanced over and recognized the two investigators from CSU hanging around the car. They'd covered the windows and windshields with a black cloth and seemed to be doing a poor job covering the entire car. "What are they doing?" she muttered.

The front passenger-side door opened, and a man came out. Vikki recognized him. It was

Dennis Mallory, head of CSU for SIPD. He was dressed in a disposable gown like the ones offered at the ME's office. He had on a face mask and wore latex gloves. In his hand was a flashlight emitting blue fluorescing color.

Vikki's heart skipped a beat. Mallory was known to be thorough with crime scenes. Had they found Hazel's body in there?

Mallory killed the blue light. He carefully peeled off one glove, then ripped off his face mask. "That is no crime scene.

It's a cesspool. I wouldn't get in that car even if I were paid." He removed the second glove. "What happened to getting a room!"

Gomez smiled and waved at Mallory, who didn't wave back. "I wonder what those lights showed? I've seen him eating a sandwich next to a vic who had his head crushed by an eighteen-wheeler. I know he'd seen it all."

Jordan winced.

"He's an intellectual,' Vikki said. "He needed something more stimulating."

Gomez opened his mouth.

Vikki glared at him. "Don't go there. Wrong choice of words."

"I can tell you what those lights showed," Jordan said, inserting himself into the conversation. "A lot of bodily fluids. I'm thinking semen. It fluoresces blue between three hundred and four hundred and fifty millimeters in the ultraviolet range. Dr. Wood discovered that in nineteen nineteen. He found—"

Vikki turned to the apartment manager. "Hold it, *Professor* Jordan! Let's discuss something more constructive. When was the last time you saw Hazel Wheeler?"

Jordan squinted. "I'm not so sure—last week or earlier in the week. I'm not always there. The video camera must have captured her in the lobby leaving or coming back." He paused, cocked his head, and massaged his chin.

"Is something wrong?" Gomez asked.

"I already saw the footage from this morning. The movers were here, but I didn't see her coming or going."

Vikki nodded. "Is this something she does often? Like, going somewhere on foot?"

Jordan gave her a look like she'd sprouted a second head. "Of course." He pointed. "There's a minimart down the alley past the dumpsters. It has a grocery store, laundromat, and salon. There's Chinese food, too. There are plenty of reasons to walk."

"Can you get to the cemetery from here, too?" Vikki asked.

"The Crawford Cemetery? Sure. It's a hike. Give or take a mile away."

Vikki remembered the arch over the graveyard. "No, St. Ives Cemetery."

Jordan chuckled. "They changed the name. I think it used to be the burial spot for the Crawfords, one of the early settlers in the area who struck it rich. Like other multi-millionaires from the gilded era, their offspring had difficulty paying taxes on those huge properties, plus the high mainte-nance costs. They sold the cemetery to the city for a token. I think they kept the house."

"You like filling your head with...things, right?" Gomez said. "Why don't you show us your video feed and walk us through it."

"Yes, you can say it," Jordan said. "Filling my head with useless information."

Vikki turned to the uniform and apologized. "He's all yours after we're done with the videos."

"No worries, Detective."

Gomez nudged Jordan on the shoulder. "Lead the way."

"Sure, we'll have to go back inside," Jordan said. "But, what's this all about?"

"We're investigating a homicide," Vikki said. "That's all we can tell you. It's an ongoing investigation."

"I know. I watch *Law and Order*."

Jordan's office was behind the locked door close to the mailboxes in the lobby. Inside, the office was small, clean, and tidy. It had a chair, table, and computer textbooks stacked on the floor.

Four monitors showing different perimeters around the

building were suspended on a tree-branch-like monitor stand. One showed the parking lot and the alley in the back. Another showed the lobby and the entrance to the building. The third, the laundry room, and the fourth, rotated views from other cameras.

Jordan pulled out a chair. "I hope you don't mind if I sit."

"Go for it," Vikki said.

He typed out commands on the keyboard. "I've already seen the footage for today. She wasn't on it. The homicide you're investigating, what day did it happen?"

Vikki hesitated. "Tuesday night."

"Let's start on Tuesday morning then, like seven a.m. I'll speed it up."

The video showed apartment residents coming down or going up, like in a Chaplin movie. For a security camera, it was clear. As it sped up to afternoon, there was no sign of Hazel. Now and then, Jordan did a cameo—appearing for a short time.

"Is there a back door?" Gomez asked.

"Yes, but this gets the least traffic."

Vikki saw a woman in black come down the stairs. "There! Freeze it."

Jordan paused it. She was dressed in black, similar to what Cindy wore. On her chest was a large cross pendant.

"Can you play it in slow motion?"

Jordan did. They watched Hazel cross the lobby with a handbag over her shoulder and disappear through the front door. The timestamp time stamp was ten minutes past ten in the evening. She'd shown for less than three seconds.

Gomez leaned forward. "Can you play it again?"

Vikki leaned forward, too. "What did you see?"

"Focus on her right hand," Gomez said. "There's something there."

Hazel appeared again. Vikki's pulse raced. It was unmistakable. In her right hand was a stake.

"My God," Vikki whispered. "She did kill her."

Jordan pointed at the screen showing the alley. "Hey, what's going on over there?"

A woman appeared to be screaming. The uniform ran toward her.

Vikki sprinted for the door.

CHAPTER SIXTEEN

Vikki slowed when she got to the parking lot, her hand resting on her Glock. She looked around—there was no active threat. She was out of breath when she got to the officer and the woman from the video.

"Acosta...what's going on?" Vikki blurted. Her breath came out in gasps, each one forming a mist in the cool air.

"She opened the dumpster to drop her garbage and saw a woman there," Acosta said. He faced the woman. "Calm down."

"Calm down?" said the woman, screeching. "I just saw a fucking dead body!"

Vikki glanced at the dumpster. There was a garbage bag on the floor. "Did you check it out?"

"I got the information from her. I thought she was hurt," Acosta said.

Gomez arrived and stood beside Vikki. His breathing sounded like a buffalo.

"The lady saw a body inside the dumpster. I'm going to check," Vikki said. She extended a hand toward Acosta. "Lend me your flashlight."

Vikki was walking away when Acosta called for an ambulance. She pulled out latex gloves from her pocket and snapped them on. This was a potential crime scene. The dumpster was large and deep with a plastic cover.

She heard movement behind her and whirled. It was Gomez. "I didn't know you were behind me." She lifted the lid and flashed the beam, ignoring the choking smell of decaying garbage.

The body was female, clad in black, partially covered by garbage bags—a stake sticking out of her chest. Vikki swallowed. She moved the light up to the woman's face. Her fears were confirmed. Hazel Wheeler's eyes stared, unblinking, into space.

Vikki's stomach churned. She stepped back. "It's Wheeler." Her voice was barely audible.

Gomez gave her an incredulous look. He fished out his cell phone from his pocket, tapped, and swiped on the screen. The light came on. He lit up the dumpster and exhaled loudly through his mouth.

Vikki unclipped her radio from her belt and spoke with the dispatcher. She gave her badge number and the location. She walked back to Acosta. "You can secure the scene. I'll stay with her."

Vikki turned to the lady. She was African American, full-figured, and probably in her thirties. "I'm Detective Victoria Mattsen. What's your name?"

"T-Teri...Teri Smith," said the woman. Her lips quivered as she spoke.

"Teri, I know you've already told Officer Acosta a lot about tonight. Can you tell me again what happened?"

"Nothing happened!" Teri said. She was clearly distraught and afraid, but tried to hide it with anger. "I came out to throw out my trash. I opened the dumpster and put it in, but the lid didn't shut all the way. I didn't want to be the one leaving the lid open and inviting rats. I grabbed the bag, tossed it to the left, and saw her." Teri sobbed. "Those eyes will haunt me for the rest of my life!"

"Do you know her?"

"Know her?" Teri said. "I didn't stay long enough. Once I realized what I was seeing, I fell back."

Vikki glanced over and watched Acosta set up a perimeter with yellow tape.

Blaring sirens got louder and louder. A car screeched to a halt, and Mallory got out. They must have heard on their way back to the station and turned around.

One of the investigators popped the trunk and gathered what they needed, including temporary lights. Soon they were doing what they did best, investigating a crime scene. Mallory would let them know once he had a theory.

More cruisers arrived at the scene. Vikki waved Acosta over to let him continue with the interview.

Gomez walked up to Vikki. "I walked down the alley, and you could get to any part of America from there."

Vikki knew what he meant. Anyone could come and go. She stepped away from Acosta and Teri and wondered if there was CCTV along the route that captured the crime. "Did you see any cameras?"

Gomez shook his head.

"I think she was murdered somewhere else and put in the dumpster," Vikki said. "But somewhere close by." She raised her head. "You saw the stake?"

Gomez nodded. "In the video, she had it with her..." His voice trailed off.

Vikki took a deep breath and let it out through her nose in a rush. "Hazel couldn't have killed Cindy. The time stamp on the camera was five minutes after ten. Cindy was murdered between seven and nine."

Vikki turned around. "Where's Jordan? Maybe his cameras caught something."

Gomez pointed toward the front of the building. "Over there."

Jordan stood there lost. They walked over to him.

"We have to look at your cameras again," Vikki said.

Jordan glanced around as if searching for answers. "You found a dead body?"

"Yes, come on, let's get back in," Gomez said. "This time, we'll focus on the rear cameras."

CHAPTER SEVENTEEN

Inside Jordan's office, Vikki and Gomez were glued to the monitor, eyes peeled, watching the reels go by.

"I can't believe you didn't have a camera fixed on the dumpster," Gomez said after they'd been watching for about sixty minutes.

Jordan, who had regained some of his composure, threw out his hands. "A dumpster is where you put unwanted, undesired material and waste products discarded by residents. Who would want to protect that?"

"What about making sure that your tenants are safe at night," Gomez shot back.

Jordan folded his hands over his chest. "I'll put a camera there once this is over. It's not my fault the body dumping was out of camera range."

Vikki turned to Jordan. "Repeat the last sentence."

Jordan hesitated. His eyes darted from Vikki to Gomez and back to Vikki. "Ah...it's not my fault the body dumping was out of camera range."

"Out of camera range! What if the perp accosted her in the alley? We should watch closely for signs of struggle."

They went outside to the back, politely asking Jordan to stay behind.

"This is police business," Vikki had said with a smile.

It was a beehive of activity. The scene was lit with portable lights. The parameter had been widened to keep away curious members of the public who lined up the outside the yellow line. The ME's van was parked close to the dumpster. So was an ambulance. An EMS personnel was talking to Teri.

Vikki glanced around, hoping to catch a glimpse of Ted despite the emergency. Her heart longed for him. Gomez spoke and pulled her out of the deep hole she was about to fall into.

"What do you think about him, Jordan?" Gomez said.

"It crossed my mind he could be the killer, but he appeared on the screen several times. When we get a time of death, we can see if there are any gaps." Vikki woke up her phone with a tap. "Wow, look at the time. I can't believe we've been here for more than an hour. Let's see if the ME has a time of death."

"I'll check on Mallory to see if they have a theory," Gomez said and peeled off.

Vikki walked up to the bin. Three individuals in protective gear and face masks hovered around. She ID'd Ted from his size and physique. "Dr. Brandon."

He turned, and the corners of his eyes crinkled. "Detective, good to see you. You caught us right on time."

Vikki nearly rolled her eyes at the charade. But it was she who'd insisted on it. It amazed her how pathologists appeared unfazed by human tragedy. To them, it was another day at the office. "Do you have a time of death?"

"The MO is similar to the victim from the cemetery. Little bleeding from the spike and discoloration around her neck. I think she was strangled." He let out a breath. "Time of death—I'll say about forty-eight hours ago based on rigor mortis and blowfly activity. When I get her to the lab, I will get a better approximation."

Vikki knew little about forensic entomology and insects' role in pinpointing the time of death. She was open to learning more. "Blowfly?"

"They're insects that lay tiny eggs in batches, in wounds and orifices. They hatch into larvae in as little as fourteen to twenty-five hours. They feed for a few days as the pupa and later adult, and the cycle is repeated. Based on the stage of colonization, the time of death can be deduced."

"We might have a serial killer on our hands," Vikki said.

Ted shook his head. "Not until there's a third victim."

They gazed at each other. Then the spell broke.

"I have to run. We have our pictures. I'll work on the autopsy later tonight once the body is released to me and let you know any pertinent findings." He made a kissing sound.

Vikki felt hot all over. She muttered to herself as she strolled over to Mallory and Gomez. "Focus, Mattsen, you have a killer on the loose." She noticed yellow cardboard on the ground.

"Hello again, Detective," Mallory said when Vikki walked up. "Unlike the case earlier, this is a challenge. So much so that we have no smoking gun. She was probably killed somewhere else and dumped here." He pointed at Gomez. "Mike says there's nothing on camera either."

Vikki nodded.

Mallory continued. "I can tell you that the doer is physically strong. It was a surprise attack. I think she was walking and was grabbed from behind around the neck. He held on and continued squeezing until she was dead. It's like a lioness in the Serengeti. Once they bite an antelope's neck, they hang on until the animal goes limp."

Vikki pointed at the yellow card. "What is that?"

Mallory came over. "He laid her down here and drove the stake into her chest. Then lifted her in front of him and dropped her into the garbage." He nodded. "Very strong." He removed his gloves and let out a sigh. "I have to go. It's been a long night."

"Thank you, Dennis," Gomez said.

Mallory headed for their car.

"Excuse me, Detectives," said a voice behind them.

Vikki and Gomez turned. It was Officer Acosta.

"John. You're still here?" Vikki said. "I thought you went with Teri to the hospital."

"No, she declined any treatment. She said meditation and a few glasses of wine might help her unsee what she saw."

"What's up?" Gomez said.

"You have to hear this," Acosta said, heading down the alley. "I saw this homeless man settling down for the night. I told him this was a crime scene, he couldn't stay. He said he knew. That he saw it all, and would I leave him alone if he told me what he saw? I said maybe."

"It was a werewolf," said the homeless man. His voice was gravely and thick. "I lay here trying to sleep. The girl strolled past—smelled good, all flowery. Then he followed, messing up the air. He walked like a man dipping his shoulder with each step. He grabbed her from behind and didn't let go until her kicking stopped. I smelled urine. Something dropped from her hand. He carried her over to the dumpster and laid her down. He came back. I thought he was coming for me."

"Did he see you?" Vikki asked.

"I can't say. But I knew I had no quarrels with him. He picked up what she'd dropped and stabbed her with it. He yanked off something around her neck, then tossed her into the dumpster."

"What happened next?" Gomez asked.

"Hmm, I guess he went home."

Vikki's mouth dropped open. For a second or two, nobody said anything. She raised her hands above her head and let them drop to her side. "Why didn't you call the police?"

"As I said, I had no quarrels with him. And I like keeping my nose on my face, not in other people's business."

Vikki exhaled. "Can you describe him?"

"He was hairy all over. He looked like half man, half wolf."

"A werewolf, right?" Gomez said.

"Exactly."

"Have you been drinking, sir?" Vikki asked.

"Yes. It doesn't affect my sight, only my equilibrium. I know what I saw—half man, half wolf."

CHAPTER EIGHTEEN

Vikki dropped Gomez off at the PD so he could get his car. By the time she was driving home, the time was ten forty-five p.m. Her cell phone rang. She glanced around to ensure no deer were lurking along the road waiting for the right time to dash in front of her. Once beaten, twice shy. A few months ago, they'd done exactly that.

It was Angie, her reporter friend. "Hey."

"Vikki, why are you holding out on me?"

"I'm doing well, Angie. How are you?"

"Unbelievable! Vikki, when were you planning on telling me?"

"Angie, I have no idea about what you're talking about. Tell you what?"

"Come on, don't play that game with me. I have a story ready to go, and you haven't called to give me a hint."

Vikki took a deep breath and let it out slowly. "Angie, calm down." Vikki hated using that word when people were upset. She spoke slowly. "Why don't you tell me what this is all about." Angie drew in a deep inhale and let it out noisily.

"Okay, it's rumored that a second body was discovered inside a dumpster. The second victim of the werewolf. And I—"

"I left the crime scene about thirty minutes ago. The werewolf connection was mentioned by a drunk. Which I thought was madness. My goodness, who told you about it? Gomez?"

He wouldn't have time for that. Maybe it had been Acosta.

It was Angie's turn to be quiet. Vikki felt her silence like heat from an out-of-control bushfire. She was a journalist. She must have her sources.

"You didn't know about it?" Angie asked.

Vikki shook her head. Remembering Angie couldn't see her, she said, "No, it's new to me too." Vikki sighed. "Okay. A girl was murdered in the cemetery on Tuesday night with a stake driven through her heart. We didn't know what to think, considering it was almost Halloween. Our investigation led us to her friend as a person of interest. Then we find the girlfriend murdered in the same way."

"A spike to the heart, too?" Angie said.

Vikki felt she'd already given too much information to someone not part of the police investigation. What was one more piece of info? "Yes. As we were wrapping up, this homeless man who had been drinking said he saw the whole thing —a werewolf did it. And now you're repeating it."

Angie chuckled. "Two coincidences make a fact."

Vikki had neutralized her attack with a dig. "So, what did you hear?"

"Well, as you know, I'm an investigative journalist, and I investigate—"

"Angie, cut the bullshit."

"Vikki, it's no bull. I heard about the murder and put it on my blog on the *Chronicle's* website. People commented that they'd seen a werewolf in the cemetery at night over the years. It was only a matter of time before it claimed a victim. And it seems that the time has come."

"How many people said that?"

"Maybe one," Angie said in a whiney voice. "She was passing by at night and saw him in the cemetery. When I directly messaged her for an interview, she said, 'No way.'"

Vikki's thoughts raced. Was it possible? A werewolf. Half man, half wolf. The drunk mentioned it with full conviction. Mallory had said whoever killed them was strong. Werewolves were supposed to have manic strengths. Vikki couldn't help herself. She laughed.

"You find it funny?" Angie asked. "I thought so, too, until I heard about the second killing."

Vikki got herself together. "Maybe we have a nutcase trying to pull a reversal. Think of Dracula."

"But he was affiliated with bats, not wolves," Angie said.

"Okay, what I'm trying to get at is people kill vampires by driving a stake through their hearts. Now we have a werewolf driving a stake into vampires' hearts."

"Maybe there's a feud going on between vampires and werewolves," Angie said. "A paranormal fantasy book plot come to life in Jersey."

They both laughed.

Vikki drove into her apartment's parking lot and pulled into a spot. Her expression was back to serious.

"Angie, I just got home. It's been a long day. Two people are dead. Angie, what you told me, excluding the werewolf, is correct. Please don't mention the second victim's name. We haven't notified the next of kin yet."

"Sorry I yelled. I didn't mean to."

Vikki saw an opening. "So, who's your source in the police department?"

Angie chuckled. "I'm sorry, but not that sorry. Have a good night."

Vikki planned to. She took a shower, turned off the ringer on her phone, and went to bed.

CHAPTER NINETEEN

Vikki got to the police department Thursday morning before nine a.m. She wore a grey pantsuit, a black blouse, and a peacoat.

Something was going on. Jody was at her desk and on the phone, talking. She looked through Vikki as she walked past her desk.

She took the elevator and got to the squad room. There were more detectives there. It was like the night shift had stayed back. John Wu came by.

"Detective Wu," what's going on?"

John was a friend of hers. He'd returned from vacation not too long ago and was always ready to lend a helping hand. She'd added "detective" to get his action and a reaction from him.

"Hi, Vikki. What's up with the detective?"

"Sorry, everybody seems in a hurry. What's going on?"

"I think it's about your case. The chief is hopping mad."

Vikki's insides tightened. "Levin?" Her mouth went dry. "What happened?"

John Wu glanced around. "It's in today's *Chronicle*—a

crazy story. You'll have to read it for yourself. Anyway, I have to go."

Was it Angie's story? Vikki continued to her desk. Someone had left a copy for her. Was McClane up to his old tricks again? She saw the headline and froze. She started to read.

A werewolf in St. Ives, New Jersey? By Angela Baxter

What is going on in St. Ives? Is it the new location for filming Stranger Things? Every other day someone is murdered in this picture-perfect town of beautiful lakes, old farms, and cemeteries. Yet, the unthinkable occurred in one of these peaceful and serene atmospheres.

A young woman dressed as a blood-sucking vampire on her way to a Halloween party was brutally attacked and murdered. Two days later, the body of another young woman was found. Both were taken from us prematurely in the most gruesome way.

Who did this? The suspicions are hair-raising. Eyewitness accounts who refused to give their names said that a creature we read about in the realms of fantasy was seen walking away from each scene.

It makes one wonder if we live in the greatest country in the world or fifteenth-century Romania, in the court of the Wallachian noble, Prince Vlad the Impaler, aka Dracula.

Or is there a killer amongst us? An extraordinary killer. A man by day and wolf at night—a werewolf? Were the women vampires for real? Or was this something else?

Vikki heard approaching footsteps and looked up. Gomez walked in, holding a copy of the *Chronicle*. His face was as tight as the Gordian Knot. Captain Levin followed. A few more detectives came in. Some uniforms stood outside the door. A hush fell across the squad room.

The chief began. "Ladies and gentlemen. You've all heard what's going on. We have a killer on the loose at a critical time in our community. A time when our loved ones get a chance to dress up and get to know other people in the community they live in by trick or treating."

Vikki's gaze was fixed on him. Her heart was galloping like it wanted to escape from her body. Captain Levin raised the newspaper in his hand, and Vikki's heart sank. He knew Angie Baxter and Vikki were friends. Was he going to call Vikki out, asking how her friend knew this?

"The newspapers think there might be something special about who we're dealing with," Levin said. He scanned the room.

Vikki wanted to say, "A werewolf—a creature of mythology. But rest assured, there's no truth to this. This individual, male or female, is nothing more than another low-life criminal, just like the rest. A coward who hides under the cloak of darkness to murder women and terrorize children." But, she remained silent.

"I called you guys in here this morning, so all hands will be on deck as we fish out the person or persons responsible for this. The mayor is under pressure to cancel Halloween. Jody, our admin secretary, has been fielding phone calls from the public all morning. Their major concern is: is it safe to go trick or treating?" He paused and looked some of the people in the room in the eye.

Vikki glanced around, too. People were focused.

"We cannot be the St. Ives Police Department that Halloween was canceled under our watch. We must find the perps before they cause more damage. Those who can sign up for overtime, please do. If you can't, keep your eyes open wherever you are. If you see something..."

The group replied as one, "Say something!"

"Thank you very much," Captain Levin said.

Vikki let out a breath of air about to pop out of her ears.

People started to disperse.

"Mattsen, Gomez, to my office," Captain Levin said and strolled past them.

CHAPTER TWENTY

Captain Levin lifted his cell phone to his ear and entered his office. He waved them to a chair and took a few steps to his favorite window. From the one-sided conversation Vikki could hear, it seemed like a family friend wanted to know the position on Halloween from the horse's mouth.

"No, it hasn't been canceled," Captain Levin said. "We're working hard to bring in who's responsible."

There was talking from the other end of the phone.

Levin nodded. "I'll let you know if anything changes." The frustration was evident in his voice. "Bye." He turned to them.

"Mattsen, your friend has put the whole town into panic. Was that story worth it? I hope she gets more than a pat on the back." He looked at Gomez and smiled. "At this rate, Mike, you're never going to retire. You'll stay on like me."

Gomez chuckled. "No, I'll reach out and take you with me. Mattsen is overripe to kick me to the curb and run the whole thing alone." He sighed. "I heard about this werewolf thing last night." He glanced at Vikki. "It sounded like something out of a Brothers Grimm story. And it didn't help that the homeless man telling the story was a drunk. It's hard to believe. I don't know what is going on, but I'm sure there's a logic to this."

"Mattsen, what do you think?" Captain Levin said.

"I'm with Gomez. The stories sound bizarre, but until we get to the bottom of it, we wouldn't know."

The chief nodded. "I think you should focus on the first, Cindy Kent. I'll put a second team on the Hazel Wheeler. I want results fast. Maybe revisit the leads you've already cleared. Look at them again and hold their feet to the fire if you have to."

Gomez, sitting beside her, inhaled and exhaled noisily.

Captain Levin continued. "I'll suggest revisiting where she worked again. She leaves work and gets murdered. Interrogate the staff again. Visit every home and business along the route she took. There must be something."

Vikki didn't like being given paint-by-number instructions. She was going to do all that anyway and would bet a dollar Gomez didn't appreciate it either. He shouldn't be treating them as rookies.

Captain Levin strolled to his chair. "Anyway, that's about it. Suppose you need more people for surveillance, anything. Let me know, and I'll assign someone right away."

Vikki and Gomez got up and left the office.

Gomez shut the door and said, "I get the *Chronicle* at home. I saw the article before I left. This is crazy. I'll be right back. I want to read the statement Acosta got from the homeless man last night."

"Good luck with that," Vikki said, returning to her desk.

She sat and shut her eyes. Where should they start? Why had Cindy worked in a restaurant and Hazel in a massage parlor? Brian Davis, Cindy's boyfriend, had been ruled out.

They didn't know if Hazel had a boyfriend. From what Mallory had found in the backseat of her car, perhaps she was multiamorous.

Vikki's eyes flew open. How did she forget this again? She'd wanted to notify the next of kin herself. She was sure the uniforms had done it.

The captain's instruction had been explicit—focus on Cindy alone. She got a pen and paper and started a list. Find Cindy's next of kin. Done. Boyfriend? Check. She tapped the pen on her lip. What did the two girls have in common? A similar outfit was bought from the same store.

Vikki woke up her iPhone and went to the photo album. She swiped until she got to the picture of the receipt from Hazel's apartment. She'd bought a mystery bag. What was a mystery bag? Vikki knew of mixed bags. She pinched her lips as she thought. An assortment of things in a sealed bag. Maybe they should go back to Franklin. It was morning, and she was sure the store wouldn't be as busy as the last time they'd been there.

Gomez returned—his Gordian-Knot-like face was back in place. "Can you believe it? The homeless man ended the conversation after we left. And there was no coffee." He flopped into his chair. "All those dicks working overtime are getting more money and drinking all the coffee, too."

"If you're only pissed about coffee, we'll get some on the way."

"On the way to where?"

"Back to the costume and consignment store in Franklin."

Gomez glanced at her. "Something new came up?"

Vikki passed her phone to him. "The receipts from Hazel's apartment. We've seen the dress but not what the mystery bag held. It could be anything."

Gomez nodded and gave her the phone back. But he still

wasn't happy. "We'll have to find whoever is responsible for this." He shook his head. "My Halloween party must go on, and people must attend. I need to show off my sword."

Vikki shrugged. "Sure. Let's go to Franklin. The party must go on."

CHAPTER TWENTY-ONE

Vikki was surprised when they pulled up at Authentic Costumes. Finding a parking spot was as complex as the night they'd been there previously. The only difference was nobody was milling about or resting on the hood of a car. "People are still getting ready for Halloween."

"Didn't they read *The Chronicle* this morning?" Gomez said.

Inside the store, it was busy. The mechanical sounds were there, but the carnival effect was gone, though there were still a good number of people.

Vikki spotted Bill, the store owner, in the customer service section. Today he wore the costume of a mad scientist. Gomez led the way. Bill finished with a customer, and it was now their turn.

Bill smiled. "Detectives Gomez and Mattsen, good morning. I must have made an impression that you guys came back."

Gomez glanced around. "Business must be booming. I didn't expect to see this many people during the day."

Bill nodded. "As Halloween approaches, procrastinators and the FOMO folks turn out en masse."

Gomez chuckled. "I used to be in the *fear of missing out* crowd. But not anymore. It's so exhilarating buying your costume early."

Bill smiled and leaned forward. "I'll let you in on a secret." His voice was a whisper. "Since the article this morning in the newspaper, our vampire and werewolf costumes have been flying off the shelves. I just reordered."

"I thought it would be the other way round," Vikki said.

"Morbid fascination," Bill said. "I guess it's the same reason something unexpected goes viral and a well-thought-out campaign doesn't. So, how can I help you?"

Vikki was about to show him her phone screen, then changed her mind. "We're investigating the second homicide, since it seems connected to the first."

Bill shook his head, putting on a sad face.

"Both women probably were here together the last time. I found a receipt that said Hazel Wheeler bought a mystery bag. What is that?"

Bill placed a hand on his chest. "Phew, you had me worried for a second. I thought we broke the law or something. Okay, a mystery bag is a way of listing things I came up with. As you know, I also run a storage facility. When payment lapses for a storage unit, we follow the laws of the land and try to get in touch with the unit owner first. After thirty days, we put a lien on the contents."

Vikki got a fluttery, empty feeling in her stomach. This case was about to get wings.

Bill opened up his palms as if lecturing a class. "If we cannot contact the owner, the contents go to auction to cover the amount owed. Whatever is left is kept for the owner."

"And since the owner never showed up in the first place, what happens to the money?" Gomez asked.

"We turn it over to the state," Bill said. "The state keeps it under the person's name and social security number. So, it would pop up whenever the person or their estate accesses the found money website."

Vikki's pulse picked up a notch. She swallowed. So, the bag had been auctioned off from somebody's unit. "Do you know what was in the bag Hazel bought?"

"No, and neither did she before she bought it." Bill drew in a deep breath and exhaled. "They'd finished with the costumes and heard the auction. That piqued their interest. 'What's going on there?' she'd asked. I said it was a mystery auction and explained what it was. We don't know what's in the bag. Nobody would bid on it if we opened it, and they're just rags."

A woman wearing the store's tee shirt approached the counter and raised her hand.

Bill faced her. "One second." He refocused on Vikki. "I said to her, take a chance. It might contain a million dollars in jewelry, and it's yours to keep. She asked if she could bid, and I said why not. I think she paid ten dollars. Is it somehow connected to what's going on?"

"That's what we're trying to find out," Vikki said. "Do you by any chance know who the unit belonged to?"

"Not off the top of my head, but I can find out."

The employee raised her hand. "Excuse me, sir."

"We're kind of swamped right now," Bill said. "Give me your number. I'll look it up and call as soon as I can."

Vikki gave him her card. "Thanks for your time."

Gomez gave Bill his card, too. As they walked to the car, he said, "It'd be sad if a bit of excitement cost them their lives. Let's head over to Mike's Diner."

CHAPTER TWENTY-TWO

It took Vikki and Gomez an hour to cover half a mile on a windy, hilly road. Road construction sprang up, then an accident. It was probably caused by motorists surprised by the sudden appearance of a road maintenance crew.

It was one of those tight spots where there was no place to go, even when you had a siren. The uniform asked one side to move while the other waited. Gomez was pissed.

Then when the accident was cleared, and the line started to move, the middle school let out, compounding the problem. Suddenly, the endless string of yellow buses was prioritized.

At Mike's Diner, Vikki slipped into a booth.

Gomez headed for the bathroom. "I'll be right back."

Vikki started at the menu with her mind elsewhere.

Gomez returned rubbing his hands together. He called for the menu. "The effects of anger or hunger can be countered by alcohol or soul food. Since I can't drink on duty, I'll eat!"

Vikki sighed. If you can't beat them, join them. She was famished. "Bring a second order of whatever he wanted." When the food came, all Vikki said was wow. She probably wouldn't eat for two days after that. It was a double cheese-burger with large, seasoned fries and chicken tenders.

They ate in silence. Gomez went at his food with vigor. She picked at the tenders. Watching Gomez eat filled her up. It was only when he'd finished eating that color returned to his face.

Mike, the owner, came by their table. "I hope you enjoyed your meal, Detectives."

Vikki expected Gomez to say that even cardboard tasted good when you were hungry. Instead, he gave the food a thumbs-up.

Mike beamed. "I took special care in creating it." He shook his head. "We're still hurting from what happened to Cindy. How's the investigation going?"

Vikki was cautious. Only immediate family members of the vic were told about recent progress in an investigation. She'd consider him family since Cindy worked here. "We're making little headway. Most of the time, crimes are not solved as fast as they are on TV. You find a piece of evidence and follow it for a while, leading nowhere. And you're back to square one."

Vikki remembered the man who'd stood up for Cindy the last time they'd been there. "What about the man sitting over there the last time?" She pointed. "Has he continued coming? He said he would stop if you fired Cindy."

Mike glanced at where she pointed, then back at her. His face was blank. "Who?"

"I think you called him Mel?" Vikki said.

"Oh yes. I remember. He was here that sad morning. Has he been coming? The answer is yes and no?"

Gomez's eyes darted to the ceiling and back. "Are you going to call us back with an answer?"

Mike's forehead furrowed. "What do you mean?"

Gomez went into a mini rant. "We saw this guy at the

auction place and asked him a question. He said he'd get back to us. We asked you a question. You gave us two answers."

Mike laughed. "I can explain. He doesn't visit but still orders his food—two of everything. We signed up for Door-Dash a while ago. It has helped people who don't want to come in. Our sales exploded, too."

Vikki wanted to ask why Mel bought two of everything and decided it sounded silly. Maybe he had it for lunch.

"So you guys met Bill in Franklin," Mike said. "I love those mystery bags."

"But you might end up buying junk," Gomez said.

Mike smiled. "That's the beauty of it. The thrill. It's like buying a lottery ticket and checking to see if you won. You rarely win the jackpot, but now and then, you win four or ten dollars. The rush you feel when your numbers match is similar to a mystery bag. Most of the time, you're getting someone's junk, but now and then, you get a gem. Like..." His voice choked. "Like the earrings Cindy had on that day. She said Hazel bought a mystery bag, and they were in it."

Vikki's heart hammered. She took a deep breath to calm herself. "Can you describe them?"

Mike sniffed. "Sure, large black crosses. They were light in weight but reflective. She loved them. They went with her outfit."

Vikki's pulse raced. It. Were they a match to the pendant Hazel was wearing in the video? Part of a collection. She couldn't remember if Hazel had it on when her body was discovered. She remembered Cindy had ripped earlobes. She turned to Gomez to ask him, but he asked Mike a question.

"The guy, Mel, what does he do?" Gomez asked.

"He's a writer. He writes historical fiction. I can't say how well he sells. There's also family money. The family goes back a long way. They used to own all of this part of town."

"Ah, the Crawfords," said Gomez. "Crawford Cemetery, now it makes sense. Modest guy."

Mike sighed. "I'd love to stand and chat, but I have a business to run. I'm glad we're on talking terms. We started on the wrong foot. I was upset about Cindy. Still am. I hope you find the bastard who did this."

Vikki's phone rang before she could ask her question. It was Jody from the police department. "Mattsen."

"Vikki!" Jody sighed. "Thank God I got you. The phones are going crazy. There's a Mrs. Kent here to see you."

"Can you tell her to leave a message?"

"Hold on," Jody said.

Vikki heard her talk to someone.

"She said her daughter has something to tell you about Cindy."

"Okay, I'll be there in twenty minutes," Vikki said. She turned to Gomez. "We have to get back to the PD. Cindy's sister has something to say."

CHAPTER TWENTY-THREE

Vikki asked for a to-go bag and took the rest of her food with her. Even though the road was clear, she placed strobe lights on her car. She wanted to get there as fast as possible before Mrs. Kent or her daughter changed their minds. Beside her, Gomez stepped on imaginary brakes each time they had a close shave.

Vikki and Gomez stepped through the door and entered the PD.

"They're in the conference room," Jody said. She had her hand over the mouthpiece of the phone. "The calls keep coming and coming. Is Halloween canceled? Is it safe to go trick or treating? People don't use their common sense anymore. If a killer is on the loose, you should remain indoors. I hope they have information that will help end this."

"Thank you, Jody," Vikki said and rushed for the elevator.

"I wonder what information Cindy's sister has?" Gomez asked as they rode the elevator.

"Well, find out in a few minutes."

They exited the elevator and went into the conference room. Mrs. Kent and her daughter, Kim, looked dejected. Mrs. Kent got to her feet as soon as they walked in.

"I'm so sorry for keeping you waiting," Vikki said. "We were on the other side of town. Please sit."

Mrs. Kent sat on the couch beside Kim. "Any new information? We read about the werewolf...is it true?"

Vikki had to be careful how she replied. "The person who saw it was very adamant. We're following up on that, trying to determine exactly what it was."

Mrs. Kent turned to Kim. "Tell them all that you told me."

Kim looked down at her hands. "Cin called on Saturday to find out how I was doing and what I would be for Halloween." Her voice was slow and deliberate. "I said I didn't know yet. She told me she and Hazel were dressing as vampires. They got their costumes from the Halloween store in the next town and accessories from the consignment shop next door."

Vikki wanted to ask questions but didn't want to spook the girl. She hoped Gomez wouldn't jump in either.

"Then I said maybe I should be a vampire, too. I told her about the Halloween party my friend would have at her house before trick or treating. Then she said she'd be going to a pre-Halloween party, too." Kim looked up and locked eyes with Vikki, then her eyes found her hands again. For a moment, she didn't talk.

Her mother took her hand and squeezed it. "Go ahead, honey. It's almost over."

Kim continued. "Cin said she was going to break up with her boyfriend and that she'd met another man at the place where she works. She's going to date him."

Vikki couldn't help herself. "What's his name?" She held her breath.

"Mal, no, Mel Crawfish.

"Crawford," Vikki muttered.

"You know him?" Mrs. Kent asked.

"He's a person of interest."

CHAPTER TWENTY-FOUR

Vikki assured Mrs. Kent and Kim they did right by bringing that information to them. She saw them off and returned to her desk.

Gomez was on his computer researching St. Ives.

"A John Crawford came from Scotland to the US in the eighteen hundreds," Gomez said. "He found his way to New York, then New Jersey, and got involved in mining. The family has lived there since then and became very wealthy."

"So, where does Mel come in?" Vikki asked. "Are there other Crawfords? Maybe we should be asking why he would kill Cindy if she planned to leave her boyfriend for him. Is he married?"

"Slow down with the questions. He's not married. The money is held in trust. The family tree I'm looking at is not complete." Gomez turned to Vikki. "Another question is, why kill Hazel? If Crawford killed them, what's his motive?"

"I don't know," Vikki said, shaking her head. "We can bring him in as a person of interest in two homicides. Do you remember the black cross Hazel was wearing in the video?"

Gomez nodded slowly.

"Did she have it on when we found her?"

Gomez cocked his head. "I don't recall seeing it."

Vikki picked up her desk phone. "I remember the drunk saying the werewolf snatched something from around her neck. I'll call the ME to confirm." She felt guilty. She hadn't spoken to Ted since last night to find out how he was doing. Vikki dialed the number. He'd understand.

"Hello, Dr. Brandon."

Vikki moved away from Gomez. When she spoke, her voice was almost a whisper. "Hi, it's me. Sorry I didn't get in touch earlier."

"Hey, not a problem. You have your hands full. Any progress yet?"

"Things are looking good," Vikki said. "I have a question. Hazel Wheeler. When you brought her back to the lab, did she have a necklace?" Vikki heard the beep of an incoming call. She ignored it.

Ted didn't hesitate. "No, but she might have been wearing one. There are discolorations and scratches on the skin at the back of her neck. It could have been ripped off. Is it significant?"

"I think so," Vikki said. "She was wearing one in the video before the attack. And Cindy had on earrings that were also missing. We know where they bought them from. We're hoping there's a connection."

"I'm happy to hear that. So, Halloween might still be saved?"

Vikki was distracted by the beep of an incoming call. Then the beep stopped, and Gomez's phone rang.

He picked it up and answered, "Hello."

"Vikki, are you still there?" Ted asked.

"Yes, I'm sorry, I got distracted—incoming call. Let's hope we'll nail this."

"All right, we'll play it by ear," Ted said. "Call me whenever you're free. Oh, I almost forgot. No, I didn't forget. I was waiting to hear back from the FBI before telling you. An email notification just came in."

"FBI? What?"

"I'm opening the email now. I found tissue under her nails and sent it out for DNA analysis. The mayor pulled some strings for the state crime lab to analyze it fast. Then the FBI ran it through their database. I think the result just came in."

Vikki's mouth went dry. Adrenaline rushed through her. Ted sighed, and she knew the result. She shut her eyes even before he said it.

"I'm sorry, Vikki. They didn't find a match." He exhaled. "The good news is we have the profile and can compare it against any suspects you have."

Vikki nodded. The bad news—she didn't have any. "Thanks, I have to go. Let's talk later." She hung up.

She turned to Gomez. He was on the phone and nodded a few times.

"Are you sure?" Gomez asked. "Okay, thanks so much for calling, bye."

Gomez smiled. His eyes twinkled. "That was Bill. He said he tried to reach you."

"Good thing you gave him your card, too. What did he say?"

"You won't believe it. He said the unit sold at auction belonged to, drum roll..." Gomez drummed out a beat on his table. "Melvin Crawford."

"Mel?"

"Yes. He'd paid for five years straight and refused to renew after it expired. They followed due process to the letter."

Vikki's pulse raced. So now he was trying to get them back by murdering the young women who'd bought them? She felt like yelling and bouncing from foot to foot. There was no way they wouldn't find answers with Melvin Crawford. They'd get his DNA and run it against the profile.

"So, all we have to do is get his DNA?" Gomez said after Vikki filled him in. He let out a whoop. "A cold hit, waiting to happen."

"It's time we picked him up."

Gomez typed away on his keyboard. "I think I know the address, but let me confirm with the DMV database." He paused and nodded. "That makes sense. There's a huge old mansion there. I thought it was a museum. The family, a long time ago, owned that part of town. His address is number one Old Cemetery Road, the other side of the graveyard."

Vikki got up and grabbed her coat. "Let's go."

CHAPTER TWENTY-FIVE

Vikki turned off Main Street and onto New Cemetery Road. They drove until the road became Old Cemetery Road and ended in a cul-de-sac with a huge mansion.

The wrought-iron gate was wide open, and Vikki drove into the compound. Leaves littered the driveway and lawn. Somebody was fighting a losing battle to keep the flowers and hedges in good shape.

Each time clouds moved, and the moonlight fell on the mansion, it showed its age, looking scary and foreboding, like Dracula's castle.

Vikki and Gomez exited the car and approached the stairs to the entrance. The sound of wind and leaves rustling as they rolled on the ground amplified the spooky feeling.

"Jesus, this place is scary," Gomez said.

Vikki agreed but kept her thoughts to herself. She touched the butt of her gun for reassurance and almost laughed out loud. It wouldn't be effective for a ghost.

The door was solid oak with intricate designs. Vikki searched for a bell. Finding none, she knocked.

"You call that a knock?" Gomez stepped forward and

wrapped his knuckles on the door. He turned to Vikki, eyes wide. "Jesus. It's like knocking on concrete."

Vikki tried the door handle. "Locked."

Gomez sighed, shaking his head. "There won't be any kicking down the door here. Apart from breaking a bone, I'm sure it's listed in the National Register of Historic Places. I don't want to discover what that could mean to my bank account and liberty if I'm charged with vandalism."

Vikki was quiet. She knew they were close. She could feel it in her bones. She walked down the stairs and around to the side of the house.

"Mattsen, come on. This is the one we need a warrant for. Let's go back to the office and think of something. I'm sure the captain can cash in a few favors to get a warrant."

Reluctantly, Vikki agreed. They drove off the compound and down the road.

"Mattsen, slow down," Gomez said, pointing at a lone figure entering the cemetery. "That looks like Crawford."

Vikki slowed and glanced over. The man was broad-shouldered with a thick beard. "It could be him. In silhouette, he could pass for a werewolf."

Vikki parked the car.

"Should we call it in?" Gomez asked.

"Not yet. Let's follow."

They entered the cemetery and followed him as he walked between tombs. He continued down a path, then vanished.

"Did you see which way he went?" Vikki asked.

Gomez whirled from side to side. "He was there a second ago."

A screechy sound, like a metal gate opening, reached them.

"Did you hear that?" Vikki whispered. I think it came from over there."

They crept to the location of the sound in time to see the

figure enter a mausoleum with *Crawford* written above it. It was Mel.

That section of the cemetery was familiar. Vikki realized it was the same area where Cindy Kent's body had been found. What was Mel doing in their family crypt at night?

They followed him in. Vikki was sure there was nothing paranormal about him.

The only light coming in was from the moon through windows close to the ceiling. The air was cold and musty. Mel turned right next to an above-ground tomb. They followed.

They got to where he'd made the turn, and he was nowhere in sight.

"Where did he go?" Gomez said. His voice was a whisper.

Vikki did a three-sixty. "We saw him come this way, and now he's nowhere to be seen." She glanced up. The ceiling was finished and sealed. She looked down. The floor was tiled with large squares. Vikki took out her cell phone from her pocket, turned on her flashlight and immediately saw it—a loose-fitting tile in one corner.

Gomez leaned closer. "Trapdoor?"

Vikki nodded. She was already thinking of what to slip under it and pry it up. She brought out the key to her apartment, pushed it into the edge, then beneath the tile and lifted. The tile came up, and she slid a finger in.

Vikki exhaled. "I'm going to check it out." She raised it, and to her surprise, it was a well-constructed trapdoor. It made no sound. Probably well-oiled and used often. A wooden staircase led away from the trapdoor.

She flashed the light around. Nobody was lurking.

Vikki climbed down the stairs. The bottom was a well-constructed tunnel with cement walls. She glanced at her phone. No service.

"Mattsen, I'm coming down." His voice was low and quiet.

"No!" Vikki said in a loud whisper. This could be a death trap. Gomez had a family to go back to. She thought quickly. "There's no cell phone service down here." She climbed back up to Gomez. "Why don't you call for that backup now?"

"I will," Gomez said. "But you should wait for them to arrive before going further."

Vikki acted fast. "What's that behind you?"

Gomez spun around.

Vikki pulled down the trapdoor, cutting off Gomez, and slid the barrel bolt, securing it. She was plunged into darkness.

Gomez tapped gently on the trapdoor, but Vikki was already descending the stairs. Once the stairs ended, she moved. She dared not use the flashlight. If he turned around, she'd be easy to spot. If he had a gun, that would make her easy prey. She took short, slow strides, inching forward slowly. It was the most extended shuffle for Vikki.

Her feet struck something. She stumbled and dropped her phone. Vikki was on her knees, both hands on the dusty floor, feeling until she found it. She exhaled, picked up the phone, and put it in her pants pocket.

She continued until her feet bumped into something. Probably the way up. She traced it with her finger. It was another staircase. She raised her head, squinted into the darkness, and spotted the faintest glimmer of square-shaped light —another trapdoor in the ceiling.

Vikki's pulse raced. Time to come up. She climbed up until her head butted against the basement door.

She stopped and listened. There was no sound from above. She hoped the hinges would be as silent as the one from the mausoleum. Her pulse raced. Cold sweat trickled down her back. Anything could be waiting for her.

Vikki removed her Glock from its holster and held it with her right hand. She took a deep breath, then raised the trapdoor. The hinges opened smoothly without making a noise. The room was bathed in yellow light.

Vikki was blinded momentarily. She'd spent the past twenty minutes in darkness. She squeezed her eyes shut, then opened them.

Nothing happened.

The room was wood paneled. In front of her were rows of books on a mahogany bookshelf. The spines were faded and worn, only the novel, *Dracula* by Bram Stoker, had huge legible texts on the spine. Was that the inspiration for driving the spikes through their chest?

She pushed the trap door as far as it could go, which was ninety degrees, and climbed up, holding her gun in a two-handed grip.

Vikki was halfway out of the tunnel when strong hands wrapped around her waist and lifted her out—squeezing like a boa constrictor.

CHAPTER TWENTY-SIX

Hot breath fanned against Vikki's neck. She tried to inhale—to exhale—but couldn't. *Life was being squeezed out of her.*

Vikki knew that her only chance of surviving this attack was not to let go of her Glock. Her feet touched the floor, and he snatched her up again.

Twinkling stars clouded her vision. She would black out any moment. Vikki thought about Cindy Kent and Hazel Wheeler. If she blacked out, their deaths would be in vain.

Darkness crept in from the corners of her eyes. Her body rose higher. She had only one more chance. Her friend, Alexis Devoe's face, flashed through her mind. 'You have not gotten our revenge yet.'

Vikki's body surged with renewed energy as a second wind overtook her. She had only one more act left before he squeezed her to death.

He slammed her down again.

As soon as her feet connected to the floor, Vikki scuttled backward and slammed his back into the wall. She smashed the back of her head into his face and was rewarded with a sickening crunch. His hands loosened around her.

Vikki sucked in air and drove an elbow into him as hard as she could.

His grip on her loosened.

She broke free from his grasp and dashed forward to the opposite wall.

He made a guttural sound.

Vikki whirled around, bringing her gun up.

What she saw was a face contorted with rage. Bloodshot eyes. His hands were on his face. Blood flowed down the back of his hand from a damaged nose. He released a snarl that made Vikki's blood run cold.

He charged her.

"Police! Stop!" Vikki yelled.

He did not stop. Neither did she. Vikki did what she'd been trained to do.

Three quick taps on her trigger. Then she dove.

Vikki rolled on her back and was up on one knee. Her gun pointed at the heap on the floor.

Her ears rang. She stood there, not moving. Her line of sight along the top of the Glock rose and fell with each breath. The smell of gunpowder and blood was confirmation that her bullets had done some damage. She'd check for a pulse later.

She took in her surroundings. It was a plain room with a bookshelf, a stool, and an old, framed picture of a woman possibly in her forties. What picked Vikki's interest was her jewelry. Her earrings were black crosses. Around her neck on a gold chain was a pendant—a large black cross.

The distant wailing of sirens meant Vikki's hearing was coming back. Help was on the way. She let out a huge breath and allowed her body to relax. Her lips parted in a smile. It was over.

A sudden knocking sound echoed through the stillness. Vikki jumped to her feet. Heart pounding, she swept the room, then fixed her eyes on Mel. He remained in the same position—dead. Was it her imagination?

"Boom, boom, boom!" The banging came again. Vikki zeroed in on the source—a door-shaped indent in the wood-paneled wall.

"Help me. I know someone's out there."

Vikki raised her gun and said, "This is Detective Mattsen. I'm armed. Who's there?"

"Mel Crawford." The voice was faint. "I'm locked in the closet."

CHAPTER TWENTY-SEVEN

Vikki looked at the body on the floor. Did she hear right?

The banging came again.

"This is the police. Who's in there?"

"It's me, Mel Crawford," the voice said.

"Then who's out here?"

"That's my twin brother, Marvin."

"Twin?" Vikki muttered. She examined the corpse. There were subtle differences. There and then, everything became clear to her. She fought an incredible urge to laugh. Still holding the gun, she opened the closet door.

A disheveled Mel walked out. He looked at Vikki, then the gun. His gaze went to the floor. "Oh God." He sobbed.

Vikki guessed the police were already on the property from the sirens' closeness. She made out the distinct thud of the battering ram from the myriad of voices and sounds. That door must be pretty solid. Most needed only one swing to get them open. It was only a matter of time before they reached them.

"What happened to him?" Vikki asked.

Mel glanced up at Vikki. "He has...he had schizophrenia.

He must have stopped taking his drugs. I didn't notice." He hesitated. His lips quivering, he said, "Did...did he murder Cindy and the other woman?"

Vikki nodded. Her gaze lingered on a painting hanging on the wall. "Who's the woman in the picture?"

Mel glanced up, eyes red. "Our mother. She was the one who calmed him down whenever he had his episodes. She's been dead for ten years now." He lifted his head, his expression conveying a silent 'Did you hear that?'

Above them, it sounded like a mini earthquake was happening as members of SIPD fanned out. Vikki knew she had to alert them that she was down there to avoid the risk of getting shot by friendly fire. Everyone was under tension.

"The police are here," Mel said.

Vikki put away her gun and raised her hand. "Detective Mattsen, SIPD here! The perp has been neutralized."

Movement above ceased.

"Mattsen?"

It was Gomez's voice.

A big smile stretched Vikki's face. "I'm one floor below you. Everything is under control."

CHAPTER TWENTY-EIGHT

Gomez's Halloween party was held the day before Halloween so that people with little children could still take them trick or treating.

Gomez and his wife had put a lot of thought into the party, from the assortment of foods to the smell of pumpkin spice in the home. The spice odor kept going by strategically placed burning candles around the house.

The food spread was interesting. The appetizer was mummy cheesy garlic bread. The greens were Caesar spider salad. Vikki bypassed the salad bowl. Those things looked like fried tarantulas.

The main dish was pasta—spaghetti with eyeballs. She only ate after someone said the eyeballs were meatballs with mayonnaise. Vikki swapped the apple cider punch for Hennessy and Coke.

The costumes were outstanding—many attendees dressed in vampire and werewolf costumes. Captain Levin came as himself—Navy suit with a different shirt and tie color.

Gomez beamed from ear to ear. He reluctantly retired his

gladius after it had poked some guests inappropriately. Most detectives dropped by, made a plate of food, and left. Somebody had to keep an eye on the store even though the fire was over.

Vikki walked up to the platinum blonde, about five feet and eight inches tall black woman, clad in a two-tone zip-up body suit with peplum. A pendulum-shaped fabric with a tribal print design dangled between her legs.

"Wow! Who are you?" Vikki said.

"Wakanda Forever Warrior," Angie said and sipped from her glass. She scrutinized Vikki from head to toe. She nodded. "You look sexy in your Princess of Darkness costume jumpsuit. I like the attached skirt. You should have come as an angel. You saved Halloween."

Heat rose to Vikki's cheeks, and she flapped her skirt to hide her embarrassment. "It was a team effort and luck. The spike props and werewolf sighting threw us off for a bit. Until we saw Marvin heading into the cemetery. I think he got the idea to spike them from the *Dracula* book in their study."

Angie cocked her head. "How do you know you got the right person?"

Vikki leaned back. "Excuse me?"

"What if you have the wrong person?" Angie said.

Vikki stood straight, shoulders back, chest out, and chin high. "There are no what-ifs. It was straightforward, and I'll walk you through it. Ted, the ME, recovered some tissue from under Hazel's nails. The DNA from it played a crucial role in closing the case. At first, it didn't match any on the database. But after we got Marvin and checked it against his profile, it was a perfect match."

Angie raised an eyebrow. "Really." She had an amused smile on her face. "What if I told you that identical twins have...the same DNA profile. Wouldn't that mean it could be either of them who'd committed the crimes? Think of it. According to Mel, the first time he asked Cindy out, she said no. She was in a relationship. He had no idea she was going to break up with Davis. So, because of the rejection and jealousy, he murders Cindy, then Hazel for good measure."

As she spoke, Vikki went quiet—her lips pressed together. Was the real perp running around free? A quiver shot through her stomach. She shook it off and engaged with Angie.

"Seeing their mother's jewelry on Cindy gave him a plan," Angie said. "He took it and did the same after he'd murdered Hazel. It was easy to blame his brother. Yes, we know he made sure his brother had enough to eat by buying food from Mike's Diner, but he took his meds away and let him run free through the tunnel to the family crypt." Angie leaned closer to Vikki. "Think about it."

Vikki was thinking about it, and her confidence was shot.

"There's somebody I want to meet. See you." Angie walked away.

Vikki drained her glass. She hoped the Hennessy and Coke would calm her. She looked around and saw Ted. He was dressed in an Egyptian king costume and golden wrap-around sandals. She wondered what he wore underneath the garment. But she immediately pulled my mind out of the gutter. She approached him.

He excused himself from the gladiator. "Hello, Dark One," Ted said with a bow. His voice was deeper than usual. "Something troubling you?"

Vikki repeated everything Angie had said. "Do you think Mel got away with murder?"

Ted threw out his hand. "Anything is possible, but it's doubtful. Yes, identical twins have identical DNA, but their fingerprints are different. I understand. Marvin's prints were recovered from the earrings and cross, not Mel's. Angie's playing with your mind."

Vikki looked around and found Angie by the buffet table. Their eyes met. She raised her glass.

The End

Ifeanyi Esimai is a mystery and crime writer and enjoys reading across different genres. When he's not writing or reading, he's exploring documentaries on museums and ancient history.

Click here or the image to get all ten books!

Get a FREE copy of The Rookie!

Join my reader group for updates, giveaways, teasers, and a FREE copy of the prequel - The Rookie. Click here or scan the QR code

Prologue

Marriage was a comfort but also a torment. The woman's smiling face filled the crosshairs of his scope, and his finger tightened on the trigger. The image in his scope, with some imagining, looked like the tattoo on his wrist—a skull caught within crosshairs. That was one connection he hadn't made in a long time.

He pushed the toothpick in his mouth from one side to

the other and eased off on the trigger. Another opportunity was mere seconds or minutes away. One shot, one kill. He smelled victory. The outcome was a foregone conclusion.

He had all night if he wanted it that way. This was not the Middle East or Eastern Europe, where escape could sometimes be an issue.

Sometimes he liked his job, and other times he didn't. In a way, it was like his marriage. Nobody had told him what the after-the-fact looked like. Nor let him in on the secret that two becoming one was as difficult to understand as God the father, the son, and the holy spirit being three persons in one.

He'd learned on the job, especially about the enemy within. Maybe he would have been better off never picking up a sniper's rifle or putting a ring on it. Becoming a sniper and getting married had both taken their toll on him.

Movement in the window he was watching pulled him away from his thoughts. Satisfactory execution meant he needed to know what the elements were doing—the winds especially.

His eyes drifted to the two buildings on each side of his target's home. The lights were off. They were unoccupied like the one he was in. The fireplace was asleep, and the owners were gone for Thanksgiving.

The room he'd picked was a little boy's. He had a Pikachu poster on the wall and a bookshelf with the *Diary of a Wimpy Kid* series.

He focused on the chimney of the building he was watching. It was wide awake. A mixture of black, gray, and nearly white smoke spewed from it and glided in the inky-black, cloudless sky like Dementors as if New Jersey had gone Rowling.

Should he have reconnoitered the property and gotten a little closer to figure out what glass the window was made of?

Too late now, and dangerous, too. At least he had a bullet that penetrated most surfaces.

To be doubly sure, he'd wait until his query got as close to the window as possible.

Maybe he would have had a second sniper with instant follow-up shots like in the field. But this was no field assignment. This was him getting extra credit on his own.

In his scope, the woman's face once more filled the crosshairs. He shut his left eye and took a deep breath. He let it out slowly and pulled the trigger.

"*Veni, vidi, vici,*—I came, I saw, I conquered."

Chapter 1

Vikki lay on the couch—knees bent, head resting on Ted's thigh in his apartment, feeling melancholic. She was dressed in a warm cream sweater and blue jeans. She was well protected from the cold. It'd been twelve years since that fateful day when Vikki had joined the police academy after Alexis and her dad had been murdered in cold blood. Seven, since Bruce had died in the line of duty. She wasn't there yet to forgive herself.

She sipped her prized coffee, Americano, with French vanilla syrup. It hit the right taste buds. Bitter, sweet, sour, and everything in between—precisely how she felt. She took Ted's hand and placed it on her chest.

A documentary about the Pilgrims and their interaction with indigenous people worldwide and the birth of Thanksgiving was on TV. The deep, rich voice of the presenter penetrated the thoughts going on in her head.

Ted ran a finger along her temple. "You look worried. Everything okay?"

Vikki didn't answer right away. She sat up and put her

coffee on the table. "When things are going my way, I always look for ways to screw it up."

"That's not true. Everyone has a lot of good days and one bad day thrown in. Talking can help."

Vikki inhaled and let it out with a sigh. "Today is my friend Alexis Devoe's father's birthday. Thanksgiving is always a reminder. After she and her father were killed...[Click here to continue]